Murder at the Vineyard Inn

A READ BETWEEN THE WINES COZY MYSTERY SERIES
BOOK TWO

DANI SIMMS

Chapter One

Eleanor and Samuel stood proudly at each other's side as they said their vows. The ceremony looked incredible.

In the small chapel were rows of benches decorated with the whitest lilies Avery had ever seen. Soft green accents and a softer dress code made it look truly magical. The light beamed through the chapel's stained-glass windows, painting an ethereal moment for all to enjoy.

Avery hardly recognized the town church as it was full of fresh flowers. She had also never seen Eleanor smile so brightly.

Everyone had pulled together to create a spectacular wedding. And it wasn't only the wedding that had occurred. Many festivities led up to their marriage, each one celebrating something else. There had been bridal showers and kitchen teas, and finally, the day of the ceremony had arrived, and all of them were relieved.

It seemed to Avery that the entire town had been invited. The church was packed full, and everyone watched as the couple pledged the remainder of their lives to each other. It took all her concentration for Avery not to cry.

It seemed not too long ago that Eleanor had told her how she simply wasn't interested in love anymore after her husband had died. And it wasn't long after that when she was introduced to the new town vet, Dr. Samuel Moses. Now, she stood gleaming, as she prepared to take his last name. It had been love at first sight, and the fact that they had made it to the point where they were married was no surprise to anyone.

Avery wondered if she would ever feel brave enough to look for love again. She'd lost her own husband in a boating accident, and it seemed like an impossible task to her. But it was clear to everyone present that Eleanor and Samuel loved each other deeply. So, Avery thought there might be hope for her to one day feel that kind of love again too.

A loud "AWWWW" traveled through the guests as Sprinkles carried the rings down the aisle. When Avery had first gotten him as a puppy, she wondered if he would ever learn to behave. And for the first few months, it seemed there wasn't much hope.

But after a couple of weeks of military-style dog training, Sprinkles had turned into the perfect golden retriever that she had hoped he would become. They had practiced walking that stretch down the aisle over and over again the days leading up to the wedding. So, naturally, Avery wanted to burst with pride when he did a perfect job of delivering the rings to the happy couple.

Avery waited at the back of the church, crouched low with a treat in her hand, for Sprinkles to return to her. She loved to see him with his white bow tie on and a proud puppy smile that he'd learned to give every time he'd successfully performed a new trick.

Sprinkles made his way back down the aisle toward Avery, soaking up the guests' praise as he passed them. And just as they had practiced, it seemed he would complete his task without any deviation.

That was until he got to the third row from the back. Sprinkles suddenly stopped and turned, pressing his nose against the hand of a man Avery didn't recognize. He was a tall man with thick dark hair. His suit looked as if it was just a little too tight, but purposely so.

He sported a very expensive watch, which he was careful to have on display. Everything about him seemed expensive. But what really bothered Avery was how he seemed to pay Sprinkles no attention at all. His hand rested carefully on his leg as he kept his eyes glued to the proceedings in front of him. There was something about him that seemed completely out of place. He sat upright and still as if he was poised for an audience.

Avery clicked her fingers as quietly as she could to get Sprinkles' attention. And to her surprise, it worked. Sprinkles looked at her and came walking casually down the rest of the aisle toward her, eager to receive his treat.

She looked back at the man, trying desperately to figure out who he was. But she could only see the back of his head. She did notice that he didn't seem to cheer and clap with the rest of the crowd. In fact, he didn't seem all that pleased to be there. The only movements he did make were to check that his watch was straight, his hair was neat, and his suit sat right. He reminded her of many of the businessmen she had seen during her time in the city.

The crowd cheered as the happy couple was finally pronounced Mr. and Mrs. Moses. The cameras flashed, and the crowd erupted once more as Samuel kissed his blushing bride. Soon, they were walking back toward the church doors as white rose petals rained down on them.

The ceremony had been perfect, just as Eleanor had

hoped. Sprinkles sat patiently at the doors, accepting every loving pat and scruff the guests had to offer as they left the church. His white bow tie was sitting skew, but his smile remained fixed on his face.

By the time the reception was in full swing, Sprinkles was the life of the party. He spent most of his time waltzing between tables to see who would give him the most love and the most scraps of food from their plates.

Avery wondered if there was money to be made with Sprinkles working as a professional wedding guest for other weddings in town. He seemed to be a hit.

When Sprinkles nuzzled his snout into the hand of one of the guests, it reminded Avery of the man she had seen at the ceremony. So, she looked around the room to see if she could spot him. She knew the color of his suit and figured that perhaps if she saw him from the front, she might recognize him. There were many people in attendance who had scrubbed up well. Perhaps she did know the man and simply didn't recognize him in his finest clothes.

She scanned every table and every person on the dance floor and saw no sign of his tight navy blue suit. She knew that the speeches would soon commence, so she figured she'd find him when everybody stopped moving for a moment.

"What are you looking for?" Camille asked as she took a seat.

Camille was one of the women of the Stammtisch that Avery had joined. It was a group of women that often met on an informal basis, and Avery had come to care for the group quite a bit. It didn't surprise Avery that Camille, being the quietest of the lot, would be found nowhere near the dance floor.

"I'm looking for a man I saw earlier," Avery explained. "I

didn't really recognize him from behind, so I figured I'd see if I recognized him from the front."

"That seems reasonable," Camille answered. "What did he look like from behind? Perhaps I can help you find him."

Avery was barely halfway through her description of him when Camille rolled her eyes. "That's Dean Scott," she said. "I saw him in the crowd as well, looking as sour as he usually does."

"You don't seem too pleased," Avery remarked. "I'm assuming you're not a fan of his?"

"Nobody likes him," she explained. "I'm not surprised he left early. He wasn't even really invited."

"And what exactly makes him so unpopular?" Avery asked.

"Well, for one thing, he seems to think he's better than anyone here," Camille explained. "Especially since he moved to the city."

"Oh?"

"Yes, he keeps talking about how he has this big, fancy house there, but nobody's ever been invited to it," Camille answered. "And when he does come to town to visit his mother, he invites everyone over, and then we're basically forced to hear about how fantastic his life is."

"I see. So, he's a little boring?"

"Not boring, no. He's just one of those people whose ideas will always be better than yours. If you have something, his version of it is better...he likes to pretend that he's the most important person in the universe, and the rest of us were simply placed here to remind him of it."

"Sounds terrible," Avery said quietly.

"And he's not all that obvious about it, either," Camille continued. "You don't really notice how bad he makes you feel about yourself until he's left again. He does it all with a smile and a charm that can bamboozle anybody."

"Ah," Avery said. "Sounds like he's a narcissist."

"Well, that's precisely what he is," Camille laughed. "And if you ask him, he'd tell you that it's your fault for seeing him that way."

"I understand why he wasn't invited now," Avery laughed.

Camille stretched her eyes big. "And yet, he still came."

"He would, wouldn't he?" she asked. "You know, if he's a narcissist, it would probably drive him wild that everybody else was invited except him. He probably told himself it was just an admin error or something."

"That does sound like something he would do," Camille answered, taking a sip of her wine.

Le Blanc Cellars had gifted all the wine for the wedding, and Avery was starting to worry it wouldn't be enough. In every direction she looked, she saw another bottle being opened and more wine being poured. She wondered if she'd need to get a few more cases to last them the rest of the night. But then they'd finally reached the part of the night where the music slowed, and she knew most people had likely already had their fill.

"I heard he had his mother bring him as her plus one," Camille said.

"I'm sorry?" Avery asked. She'd been so worried about the wine she'd forgotten what they were talking about.

"Dean Scott," Camille said. "He was only able to come because his mother listed him as her date."

"His mother is Mrs. Scott!" Avery said, piecing it together. "She's the lady with the rose farm not too far from here."

"That's the one! And she's even worse than he is," Camille said.

"In what way?"

Avery didn't really know Mrs. Scott. She'd just caught glimpses of her here and there in town. She was an elderly woman with sleek gray hair. She only ever wore all-white clothes, and Avery was certain she'd never seen her without her red lipstick.

"She thinks she's more important than any of us," Camille said. "She once sold roses to some or other president, and in her mind that practically makes her royalty."

Avery laughed. "How did she find herself with an invitation then?"

"She's old!" Camille cried. "Eleanor felt too bad to tell her she couldn't come, especially since Mrs. Scott insisted on giving Eleanor half-price on her bouquet. So then, Eleanor had to invite her, and then that meant Dean found a way to get himself invited too."

"Do they have a habit of doing that?" Avery asked. "You know, worming their way into other people's affairs?"

"Oh yes, they're experts at it. You've been here long enough now. It's only a matter of time before Mrs. Scott starts poking her nose in your business too."

The way the man had looked and behaved made better sense to Avery now. Everything about him stood out to her, but she understood now that it had been his intention. He had wanted everyone to notice him.

She'd known too many people like that when she lived in the city. And she wondered if he had always been that way and was sculpted by his mother's attitude or if he had adopted that behavior in the city after he moved there.

She wondered what it was about him that had gotten Sprinkles' attention. There had to be something her dog found interesting about him, but she couldn't quite under-stand what. The more she thought through what Camille had told her, the more she understood the man.

His flashy watch made sense to her, and so did his tight suit. It also explained why he didn't join in the celebration with the rest of the guests. Narcissists are most unhappy when the attention is on someone else, especially if the other person is deserving of the attention they get.

Still, there was something about him that was familiar to her.

Chapter Two

The music had changed and the dance floor was packed. In the center of the crowd danced the happy couple as they clung eagerly to each other. It was the time of the night when the music had become slower, and those dancing together had moved closer to each other.

Couples danced with their arms wrapped around each other, sneaking kisses anywhere they could. Camille had dragged Sprinkles off for a slow dance too. He'd already lost his bow tie at some point in the night.

Every guest that attended the reception seemed to have had an excellent time. It had been a magical evening, and Eleanor and Samuel looked happier than Avery had ever seen them before.

She sat on the sidelines, watching all the other happy couples dance as she contemplated all the ways her life had changed over the last few months. It was a brief moment of peace in which she thought about none of the daily stresses in her life.

But her peace was disrupted when she spotted a slightly tipsy Charles in the center of the dance floor, his arms wrapped around a half-empty bottle of merlot as he swayed his hips to the beat. Avery laughed loudly until she felt she could no longer breathe.

She'd only ever seen Charles tipsy once before, and that was at the launch party for her bed and breakfast, Cellar Vie. That night he had promised Avery he would always take care of her. She'd thought it was nothing but a silly tipsy statement, and although they'd had difficulties in their friendship, he had yet to break that promise.

She wondered what promises he was whispering to that bottle of merlot as they moved slowly from one end to the other, keeping time to the music.

Then, the music stopped. It was abrupt, and Avery worried another string of speeches would ensue. Until she heard the gasps as everybody looked toward the music booth. A group of police officers had stopped the music and were motioning for everyone to gather on the dance floor.

"What's going on?" Avery asked as she walked toward the crowd.

"Can we get everyone's attention, please?" one officer called out to them. "Gather around; it's a serious matter. We need everyone's eyes on us for a moment. We do apologize for the interruption."

Charles had been a police officer before and still worked with them as a consultant. They were good friends, and she wondered if he hadn't perhaps put them up to something as a funny prank on the happy couple. It didn't seem entirely unlike him. But the seconds passed, and nothing funny had happened yet.

It wasn't until she saw the confused look on Charles' face that she realized he also had no idea what was going on. Avery made her way over to stand next to him.

"What is this?" she whispered.

"I have no idea," he answered, placing the bottle of wine on the ground beside him.

At that moment, the door to the venue opened again, and a very concerned chief of police entered with a notebook and haste in his step. He greeted his men who had arrived before him and took his place in front of the crowd.

"Ladies and Gentlemen," he announced loudly. "I'm so sorry for the interruption, but I urgently need to inform you that all the guests who have traveled from out of town are required to stay in town until further notice."

"I don't understand," Eleanor replied. "Have we done something wrong?"

"Regrettably, there's been a murder," he answered.

There was a shocked silence in the room. Avery could feel the fear and tension on her skin. She looked at Charles and knew he had sobered up fast.

"I don't understand," Eleanor said with panic in her voice.

"We have just been to the scene of a crime where a body was found," the police chief announced. "And it would appear that the guests in this wedding are all considered suspects for now. I am sure some of you will be cleared quite quickly. But until we can prove your innocence, you will all be required to stay. Anybody who leaves will have a warrant out for their arrest."

A panicked murmur ran through the guests that still remained at the party. Avery looked to Charles as if he would have answers, but he seemed just as shocked as everybody else. She knew it had to be pretty serious if everybody was expected to stay.

"If we are considered suspects, then shouldn't we know which crime we are accused of?" Samuel asked. His face was red with frustration at the accusations.

"It is with sadness that I inform you of the murder of Dean Scott," the police chief announced. "And we are led to believe that a satchel of money has been stolen from amongst his possessions."

There was a gasp through the crowd. Avery's mouth hung open as she thought about the conversation she'd had with Camille earlier. She looked around the room to read the reactions of everybody else. If one of them could really be the murderer, then perhaps their actions could give them away.

But all she saw were pale faces and mouths that hung open just like hers. It seemed to have come as a shock to everyone, despite Camille's claims that nobody really liked him. The entire situation made her feel uneasy.

"Sorry, sir," Charles said loudly. "But what exactly makes you think that any of us could be a suspect in his murder?"

It was an excellent question, and Avery was grateful Charles had asked it. She wouldn't have had the guts to ask, and she knew it would only keep her up that night thinking about it. Then again, as a retired cop, Charles knew the right questions.

"There was evidence in the man's room at the inn that suggests he was afraid for his life," the police chief answered. "It suggests that perhaps one of the guests at this wedding intended to do him harm."

Avery's head was spinning. She suddenly remembered why the man had looked so familiar. She had seen him before at her guest house. He was one of her guests. She felt sick to her stomach at the thought of someone's murder being carried out in her guest house.

"Sorry, sir," she blurted out. "Was this at my inn?"

"At Cellar Vie, yes," he said, confirming her worst fears.

"Do I need to go there?" she asked in a panic. "Do you

need me for anything?" The police chief held up his hand to silence her.

"Your parents have been very accommodating. We'll get your statement in due time," he said. "In the meantime, I suggest you extend the stay of any other guests who have attended this wedding."

Avery nodded, but her mind was completely blank with concern.

"Right," the Police Chief continued. "Now, we ask anybody with any information pertaining to this case to please come forward."

"How could we do that?" Samuel asked, angry at the interruption. "We don't know anything about the case."

"That's true," Deb added. "All we know is that Dean was killed at the inn. We only know as much as you've told us."

"Perhaps if you gave us a little more information," Charles suggested. "If we knew which evidence it was that has made us all suspects, we might be able to help you narrow it down."

The chief of police sighed and signaled to his officers to join him to one side. They discussed it all among themselves. It was only a few seconds, but it felt like minutes that they spoke.

Avery couldn't stop thinking about her inn. She had no information. *Was it messy? Were things broken?* It seemed like silly thoughts to think when a man's life had been lost, but as a business owner she couldn't help herself.

"It's going to be okay," Charles said quietly to her. "Don't worry." And she believed him, but his words did nothing to calm her concern.

"Right," the police chief finally said. "I will share some more information regarding the case with you. Now, as you know, a large sum of money was taken from his room. We know this because he had a list of items that he had brought with him, and we found his safe open."

Avery thought she would be sick.

"It is our belief that whoever did this convinced him to open the safe before taking his life, as the safe seemed to have been opened using the pin."

Avery wanted to hold Charles' hand in case she passed out. But no matter how hard she tried, she couldn't get herself to move a single limb.

"I will read to you, now, a journal entry made by the victim. If this means anything to you with regards to who might have done this, then I insist you come forward immediately to talk to us," he continued. He held up the notebook that he'd had in his hand when he entered and began to read out loud.

I came back here to see the friends and family that I have missed. But I've only been met with unfriendliness and disgust. Threats have been made to my life, and it seems that nobody is on my side anymore.

It is clear to me now that some of the people on the guest list for tonight would love nothing more than to see me dead. But they simply don't understand me. And that is their own loss.

"This diary entry was made last night," the police chief said. "And it is considered to be very important evidence in this case." The crowd stared at him blankly as the bride and groom held each other close, their special night completely ruined. "Well," the police chief said awkwardly. "I'll let you get on with your celebrations then. Congratulations to you both."

If Avery wasn't so shocked, she might have laughed. What

a ridiculous notion that any one person present might still be in the mood to celebrate. Instead, the happy couple ended their party and went home.

Avery stayed behind as she spoke to all the guests who were staying at her inn, making arrangements for their lengthened stay. She knew she would have to leave eventually, but she didn't want to know what she would be going back to.

"Wanna share a cab home?" Charles asked as he took a seat next to her. They were the only two people still left at the venue.

"I'm too afraid to go home," Avery said, resting her head in her hands. "Do you think there'll be, like, flashing lights and tape and stuff?"

Charles chuckled. "That is probable. These things take time to clear. You'll likely find there are still a few officers around. I can only hope they've removed the body by now."

Avery groaned and lay her head down on the table. "I can't deal with that right now," she said. "It's too stressful."

Charles put a comforting hand on her shoulder. "They're going to want to ask you some questions," he said. "But I tell you what, I'll wait there with you until everyone has left. How's that?"

"You don't have to do that," she said. "You don't think they think I did it, do you?" she asked, nearly getting lost in her own question.

"It's unlikely," he said. "Besides, I'm your alibi, and I'll be right there for you."

Avery wished she could just run away and come back once it was all over.

"Think of it as character research for your book," Charles said with a smile. "It will be over before you know it."

Chapter Three

When Avery and Charles arrived back at the vineyard, Sprinkles was fast asleep on the floor of the cab. He was so tired that when Avery opened the door, he paid no attention to the flashing lights and crowd of people who had gathered. He walked straight to his bed on the porch and curled up to sleep.

Avery stared at the scene, and she felt sick to her stomach. Her property was littered with police vehicles and news crews. And as the reporters spoke, she kept hearing the name of her beloved Cellar Vie Guest House being used. It had always been intended to be a place of peace and tranquility, and now it was associated with murder.

The officers had already seen her cab arrive, so she knew she couldn't just turn around and leave again, no matter how much she wanted to. She just wished she could wait a few more hours and gather her courage.

"I don't think I can do this, Charles," Avery said, looking at the scene.

"I promise you, it won't be as bad as you think," he said

kindly. "You'll be alright. Besides, you don't have a choice. You have to approach them eventually."

There were officers and officials all over the place. Tape closed off the room that Dean had been staying in. Everyone seemed busy, and she hated to see her guest house looking that way. She had no idea what to expect when she approached the officers. But it was her home, and she knew she would have to do it eventually.

"Come on," Charles said, stepping out of the cab. "The sooner you do it, the sooner it will all be over."

She looked despairingly at him. "Can't I just wait here for another five minutes?" she begged.

"Whether you do it now or five minutes from now won't make a difference, Avery," he said with a smile. "I'll stand with you, don't worry."

He was right, and she knew it. She dragged herself out of the cab and walked as slowly as she could toward the group of officers. They had already seen her coming and turned to meet her. As she arrived to speak to them, she saw through the open door to Dean's room as they zipped closed the body bag.

"Avery, we're glad you're finally here," an officer said.

"Sorry it took me so long," she responded. "Needless to say, but I wasn't all that excited to come back to all of this."

"What happened?" Charles asked, keeping his promise as he stood at her side.

"One of the other guests phoned us when she saw that his door was hanging off its hinges," the police officer said. "While she was on the phone with us, she went inside and found him there. It's a terrible thing."

"Was she part of the wedding?" Avery asked.

"No, she's just someone passing through on her way to somewhere else," the officer stated.

"She's been a great help," the other officer said.

"Well, remind me not to charge her for her stay, Charles," Avery said. She looked at Charles and wished she could smile, but she couldn't. The stress of it all had clamped her mouth shut entirely.

"Unfortunately, we will need every copy of the key to his room that you have, and we have to ask that you allow our officers to come and go as they need for the duration of this investigation," the officer continued.

"Of course," Avery said blankly. "I only have one spare set, inside, behind the counter. I'll get it for you in a moment."

"And I'm sure I don't have to tell you," he said. "But nobody may enter that room until the investigation is over or until we officially hand it back to you with the keys."

"Naturally," Avery laughed. "Although, I think it will be a long time before I can convince anybody to go back into that room again."

She glanced back at the door as they prepared to carry his lifeless body out. She wondered what his mother was feeling. She would have heard the news by now. She could just catch a glimpse of the room, and it looked neat, apart from the broken door.

"The other officers said something had been stolen from the room," she said.

"It appears to be the case," the officer responded. "But we're working to confirm that now."

"Right, well, is there anything else I can do for you, officers?" she asked.

"You were one of the guests at the wedding, right?" the officer asked.

"We were both in attendance," Charles answered for her.

"Then you're on our list, and we need to ask you some questions," the officer said.

Avery looked at Charles in panic. She'd never been a suspect before, and it didn't feel good. Despite the fact that she knew she was innocent, there was still something terrifying about having to answer their questions.

She would tell them what they needed to hear in order to clear her name as a suspect, which would be the truth. But she knew that if she said anything even a tiny bit wrong, she would be in trouble.

"It's alright," Charles said with a smile.

"Well, unfortunately, Charles, we have to ask you to step away," the officer said. "You were a guest, and we're under strict instruction to question all the guests."

Charles was led away by the other officer, and Avery stood alone as she did her best not to look too panicked. She didn't want to look guilty.

"When did Mr. Scott first check in?" the officer asked.

"I—I'm not sure, Avery answered. I have someone who does all the checking in for me. But I have a book that should have the date. It's right there on the counter."

Another officer went up to the counter and opened the book. She took some photographs and nodded in their direction, satisfied.

"Did you know Mr. Scott?" the officer asked.

"No," she answered. "I only know of him, but I don't believe we've ever met."

"And do you have someone that can confirm your alibi for the night?" the officer asked.

Avery nodded. "I never left the wedding. I'm sure there are multiple people you can call to confirm that," she said.

"If you'd write some names and numbers down here, please," he said, handing her a notebook.

Avery scribbled down the information about the Stammtisch women and couldn't help but notice the officer cross out Deb's name. "They will have seen me there all night," she said. "I didn't leave once, not even to get some fresh air which is true of most of the guests and I'm sure I will be listed as their alibi."

"Right, well, we'll give some of these names a call in just a moment," the officer said.

"The first time that I saw Mr. Scott was today. My dog, Sprinkles, was the ring bearer, and he stopped to sniff Mr. Scott's hand. I thought it was odd of Sprinkles to do that, but no, I've never met him," she said.

She was aware she was rambling, but that's what she did when she was nervous. The flashing lights and the teams of officers were making her very nervous, and she couldn't seem to stop the words from pouring out of her mouth.

"I see," the officer said.

"But I did ask someone about him, and she explained to me that he wasn't exactly well-liked," she said. The moment she said it, she wished she hadn't. The officer straightened his back and clicked his pen.

"And who was the person you were discussing this with?" he asked. "Who told you that he wasn't well-liked?"

"Camille," she answered. "Her name is on the list I gave you."

She hadn't intended to make Camille look like a possible suspect, and for a moment, she worried they might arrest her. But she knew Camille also had a sound alibi, and it wasn't a crime to speak badly of people.

"Well, I think that's about all we need to ask you," the police said.

"Really?" Avery asked with keen eyes.

"Well, what else can we ask?" he laughed. "Do you have any questions for us?"

"How long will you all still be here tonight?" she asked. "Can I fix you all a cup of tea? A jug of water, perhaps?"

The officer laughed. "That's awfully kind of you, Avery, but no thanks," he said. "Still, you've always had a good eye for these kinds of details. If you think of anything that might be important, will you let us know?"

"She does have a good eye, doesn't she?" Charles said, joining them again. "You know she's decided to write crime novels? I think she'd be great at it."

"Yes," Avery sighed. "I figured I spend so many nights awake, I might as well put that time to good use. And my late husband wrote crime novels. I helped him a bit, so I figured, how hard can it be?"

The officer laughed. "That's excellent," he said. "You should write a story about our town. We've had a few mysteries of late, haven't we? There is enough of fodder for you here in Los Robles, what with the murder at the festival and the sad person that was discovered stuffed in the barrel."

Avery wanted to laugh, but as they carried the body right past her, she worried she might be sick. The officer who had questioned Charles joined them again.

"Well, Charles, your alibi checks out," the officer said.

"Who was it?" Avery asked. "That bottle of merlot that you were hugging on the dance floor?" It was no time for jokes, but all of them burst out laughing at the same time as Charles' cheeks turned slightly red.

"Very funny, Avery, but he's right, you know," Charles said. "This town has had some drama over the last couple of years. It might be a good idea to write about it. I think those stories would be a hit."

"That's a great idea," Avery said. "But honestly, I

wouldn't even know where to begin. I only have one perspective on all those stories, and so I run the risk of writing something that is untrue."

"I suppose," Charles said. "But that could also make it interesting."

"Oh, come on, Avery," the officer said. "There are no books about this town. I'd read it if you wrote it."

Avery looked around at the chaos that had occurred on her property and sighed. "Alright," she said. "I'll write a book about this town. But if I'm going to do it, then I'm going to do it properly. Let me write about this story." Avery motioned to the scene around them. There were people with gloves and officers taking notes. There were forensics people searching for fingerprints. It was a perfect scene for the start of a book.

"I don't know," the officer said.

"Let me follow you guys around as you work on this case, and I can use it in my book. I'll just change some of the details slightly. That way, I can call it fiction," she said.

The officers looked at each other.

"She's got a good idea," Charles said. "Don't journalists do that kind of thing all the time? What's the difference?"

"The difference is that she is, technically, still a suspect, and I need to run it by Police Chief Mathers first," the officer said.

"For how long can she still be a suspect?" Charles laughed. "You know her alibi will check out."

The officer scratched his head. "Tell you what," he said. "Because this sounds like so much fun, let me take some time to confirm you were at the wedding all night. Then, I will call Chief Mathers and see if he'll give you permission."

The officers stepped aside as they called the long list of names in their notebooks. And judging by the conversation, some of the names on that list had already been called a few times. That made sense. The guests would all list each other's names for an alibi.

Avery was sure if she checked her phone, she would have a few missed calls too.

It wasn't long before the officers came back to join them.

"Well, you're no longer a suspect," one officer said.

"That's good news, but not surprising," Avery teased.

"And Chief Mathers has agreed to let you follow us on this case for your book," he said with a smirk. "He said he's certain you'll find a way to interfere, as you usually do, and at least this way, he'll know what you're up to at all times." Charles snorted, and Avery laughed.

"That's settled then," Charles said. "Avery, are you ready to write your first book?"

Avery smiled widely in short-lived excitement. And then, the guilt set in as Avery looked at the scene. The man had been alive only hours before.

Chapter Four

It was early the next morning when Avery met the Stammtisch women to help them clean up the mess left behind by the reception. The last of the officers had only left her property well after midnight, and Avery hadn't had very much sleep.

There were bottles and confetti everywhere. The floor was covered in scuff marks from everybody's shoes, and the pile of belongings that people had left behind continued to grow. Everyone looked tired.

"How are things at the guest house?" Camille asked.

"Well, I've had to comp the stay of the poor woman who found his body," Avery said. "And cancel other bookings now that any guests who were invited to the wedding are being forced to stay longer."

"Did they give you any information on what happened?"

"No," Avery answered. "I only know what you know. But it seems that whoever did it broke the door down. I can't go near that room until the investigation is over, and I've had to hand over the keys to the police."

"That sounds like a nightmare," Camille said. "I'm sorry you have to go through all that."

"They're making it up to me by letting me follow them on the case," Avery explained. "I can use it for the book I'm writing."

They cleaned in silence for a short while until Avery found herself on the same side of the room as Tiffany.

"Are you sure you're doing alright?" Tiffany asked.

Tiffany and Avery had been friends since school, so Tiffany always knew when Avery wasn't giving the full truth. It was something that had often driven Avery a little mad.

"I barely knew the guy," Avery said. "So I don't feel too sad about it all. But being questioned like that and seeing that scene on my property was not great, and I'm very tired."

"You must be the only person in town who never knew him then," Tiffany said. "Everybody here has had a run-in with him at least once. You know, he and Deb were in a serious relationship for some time."

Deb was one of the Stammtisch women, and she was known to be the town gossip. As much as Avery loved Deb, she could believe that Deb would be involved with a man like that. He certainly had the look to match her aesthetic.

"He did look like her type," Avery laughed.

"If only he was as good inside as he looked on the outside," Tiffany said.

"Yes, I believe he was a bit of a difficult person to deal with," Avery remarked through a yawn.

"Not only that," Tiffany laughed. "He was absolutely good for nothing. I never understood why she stayed with him for so long."

"I thought he was supposed to be some kind of wealthy businessman-type?" Avery asked.

"Yes, later in life," Tiffany sighed. "But when he was with

Deb, she paid for everything while he finished his studies. Only, I don't think he ever really went to class."

"Oh?"

"Deb used to constantly complain that she would come home to find him doing nothing but lounge around on the couch. She would cook and clean and pay all the bills for both of them. She worked herself nearly to death to afford it all."

"That's terrible," Avery said. "Why didn't Deb just kick him out right from the beginning?"

"He's a charmer," she answered with a shrug. "He always seemed to convince her that his studies were more important than anything else, that she was helping him, and that it made her special to do so. I think she thought he would marry her."

"That sounds frustrating," Avery said. "What a terrible situation to be in."

"They had a horrible relationship," Tiffany continued. "They would fight all the time. He never lived with her, but he behaved as if he did. He always wanted to know where she was and what she was doing. She couldn't breathe without informing him of it first."

Avery tried to picture Deb in that situation and found it difficult. Deb was outspoken and fun and had a habit of doing exactly as she pleased all the time. Perhaps that habit only formed after her relationship with Mr. Scott.

"Where is Deb, by the way?" Avery asked. "Wasn't she supposed to help us today?"

Avery looked around the room to make sure she hadn't simply just missed Deb somewhere. But she was nowhere to be found.

"Haven't you heard?" Tiffany asked. "She's down at the police station. They took her in for questioning because of the relationship she had with the victim."

It took Avery by surprise, but she remembered how the

officer had crossed Deb's name off the list to confirm Avery's alibi. That made a little more sense to her. They couldn't phone her if she were their stronger suspect.

"Surely they don't think she did this?" Avery asked. "People break up all the time. It's normal."

"It's not because their relationship ended that they've taken her in," Tiffany said. "It's how their relationship ended; that's the problem."

They had been cleaning for hours already, and it seemed as if they had hardly made a dent in the mess. Avery and Tiffany took a break to sit outside and enjoy a cold glass of water. At that rate, they would be there all day cleaning.

"How did their relationship end, then?" Avery said, unable to get it out of her mind.

"Rather suddenly, actually," Tiffany explained. "One day, he was there, and the next, he wasn't. When she heard from him again, he was already living in his new house in the city. She simply never heard from him or saw him again."

"Sometimes it's better for things to end abruptly," Avery said. "It's easier to get over. It's when things are ugly and drawn out that the break up becomes tough."

"I suppose," Tiffany said. "But after he left, things only got worse for her because of him." Tiffany took a long sip of water and shook her head.

"About a week after he left her and moved to the city, she was trying to pay for her groceries when she discovered he had maxed out all her credit cards," Tiffany said. "She checked the statements and learned that he had furnished his new home with her money. And it wasn't cheap stuff, either."

"That's terrible," Avery said. "Surely there was something she could do?"

Tiffany shook her head. "By the time she discovered it, it was too late. And since they had been in a relationship for so long, the bank didn't want to get involved. They said it was impossible to know who was really telling the truth."

"The truth?" Avery asked.

"Yeah, naturally, when the police questioned Dean about the money he'd spent, he just told them she had spent the money on the furniture. He spun some story that they were going to move to the city together, but she dumped him at the last minute, and now she was trying to frame him for a crime he didn't commit."

"Clever," Avery said. "He knew that most banks, officers, and businesses don't want to get involved in that kind of thing."

"Precisely," Tiffany said. "They told her to hire a lawyer. But she had no more money left to do so!"

"So, what did she do in the end?" Avery asked.

"She spent years paying off that debt. It nearly ruined her completely. There was a time when she was considering selling her house to pay it off. I'm so glad she made it through all that," Tiffany said.

Avery felt sorry for Deb. But it made sense now why she would be seen as such a serious suspect. She fit the description of someone who had been seriously wronged by him. And if he knew what was good for him, he should have been concerned about seeing her again.

Avery knew Deb well enough to know that even though she had paid off the debt and made it through, there was no way she would have kept quiet about it if she had seen him. But she also knew that there was no way Deb was a murderer.

"Poor Deb," Avery said. "And now she has to go through all of this also. It's like, even in death, he's made things diffi-cult for her."

"I know," Tiffany said. "But I don't think she did it. She was at the wedding all night with us."

"Still, the police have to do their jobs," Avery said.

Avery and Tiffany headed back inside to continue cleaning up. Avery knew it was likely that they would be there all day, but she wished she could have been present for Deb's questioning. It was exactly the kind of thing she wanted to see for her book. She had promised Eleanor that she would help, and Eleanor was more important than the book. *Besides, I can't promise I won't go storming in there and come to Deb's defense. It might be for the best, after all,* Avery thought.

As she swept, she thought through all that she knew. There weren't many details, but enough to already get her mind wandering. How had he gotten away with treating her that way? How was it that nobody helped Deb get her money back from him?

"How did everybody find out about Deb's debt?" Avery asked. "I mean, I know it is a small town, but you know a lot of details about that relationship."

Tiffany shrugged. "I dunno," she said. "Everybody knew about it. It was the talk of the town for weeks after he had left her."

"That's terrible."

"Of course, everyone felt sorry for her," Tiffany continued. "And we did what we could to help. When she said she would need to sell her house, we held an auction to raise funds to help her with the debt. The whole town came together because everyone knew he was a loser."

Avery liked the thought of that. It made her feel comforted that if she should ever need the town, perhaps they would be there for her too.

"And Mrs. Scott?" Avery asked. "Could she not help?"

Tiffany threw her head back in laughter. "Are you kidding? She's just as bad as he is," she said. "The only thing she did to try to help was to offer to buy Deb's house from her. Can you imagine the audacity of that?"

"No, I can't," Avery said as she raised her eyebrows.

"And what's worse is how angry Mrs. Scott became when Deb refused to sell the house to her. She called Deb ungrateful for not taking her generous offer."

Avery wondered how she would have reacted in that situation. She couldn't imagine it, though. It seemed so unfathomable to her that someone could behave that way. Her son had stolen Deb's money and put Deb in that situation. All she could think to do was take even more from Deb and then pretend she was trying to help?

It was a ridiculous notion, but the more she thought about the descriptions of the personalities of Dean and his mother, the more she could believe it. Avery pitied Deb. It made her see her as an entirely different person, and she understood better why Deb liked to be involved in the lives of all the people in town. They had helped her out of a tough situation. To Deb, they were all her close family and friends.

"I feel sorry for her," Avery said out loud. "I hope they're not being too rough on her at the station."

Tiffany sighed. "I don't know," she said. "I think they're taking a close look at her. I mean, there were many times when Deb said she wished she could just kill him."

Chapter Five

The table was set for two as Charles and Avery tucked into their decadent grilled cheese sandwiches. It was just what she needed after spending the entire morning cleaning up the chaos left behind by the wedding festivities.

They were eating slowly as each took turns talking the other one's ear off. Although Charles worked for Avery in the wine room, he was quickly becoming one of her closest friends, and they shared a weekly meal together.

Avery loved to cook, and Charles loved to eat. So, it was an excellent arrangement. Cooking for one was a tedious task, so Avery was grateful for the weekly opportunity to put her skills to the test.

"Tiffany tells me Deb is a suspect," Avery said, chomping into her sandwich.

Charles nodded. "She's a good one, too," he said. "No, not in that way. I just mean that she'd been very forthcoming and easy to deal with. She's been happy to answer all the police officer's questions and has been very patient with them, which is uncommon in murder suspects."

"I suppose," Avery sighed. "I didn't feel all too good when

they were questioning me last night, and I wasn't even a serious suspect!"

"It's just tricky to tell sometimes," Charles said. "Some murderers are excellent liars. That's how they get away with it. And everybody knows how badly he hurt her."

Avery let out a short "mmm" as she took another mouthful of her meal. She nodded in agreement with Charles—not that she agreed with him entirely; she only partially agreed. Still, he wasn't wrong. She knew that all murderers were excellent liars, but Deb had never been able to keep a secret. She was the town gossip. It would be impossible for her to keep her mouth shut about anything.

"I feel sorry for her," Avery said. "I heard what happened. If I were here, I don't know if I'd ever have been able to look him in the eyes again."

"And that's precisely why she's one of the main suspects," Charles said. "I know she's your friend, but when it comes to murder, those things go right out the window."

"I suppose," Avery said. "I just think she wouldn't even waste her time murdering him. She's recovered and moved on. Then again, passion, and especially angry passion, makes people do the stupidest things, doesn't it?"

"Yeah," he chuckled. "By the way, how are you feeling about the prospect of writing your first book?"

"It's funny," Avery said. "I've been talking about doing it and thinking about doing it, but now the opportunity to do it has arrived, and I doubt myself."

"Doubt?"

"Well, I mean, now I actually have to do it," Avery laughed. "I have to put all those words onto paper like I've been threatening to do over the last few weeks."

Charles laughed loudly. "You're going to do great!" he

said. "It's not like you don't know anything about writing books."

"That's true," she answered. "James used to think I'd be good at it. And I used to help him a lot. I suppose part of me is afraid that I'll miss him too much."

"Missing someone hurts, but it isn't all bad," Charles said. "It depends on the reminder. Some things are a reminder of the good times, which can be comforting in the tough times. What you're doing is a happy memory you have of your husband. It will be the good kind of missing him."

Avery thought about it for a moment and decided he was right. Perhaps it wouldn't be as bad as her mind would like her to believe.

"Besides," Charles continued. "I think it will be fun to have you following the police around like that. You're going to love it. It's just like gossip but far more interesting."

"I just hope I don't get too carried away," Avery said. "The last thing I want to do is become too interfering and for them to ask me to leave them alone. I don't know if I could motivate myself otherwise."

"That is a risk," Charles said. "You haven't always been on the best terms with them. Just, whatever you do, don't have too much fun."

"Why not?" she laughed.

"I don't want you to sign up to join the force!" he teased. "It's too risky. You're one of my best friends, and I can't lose you. Who will feed me these delicious meals?"

"Oh, the horror!" she said dramatically.

"Precisely!" he joked. "If something were to happen to you, I would live off of takeout and microwave meals, and that is a threat."

"I take that threat very seriously," she answered, gathering their plates.

Avery went to the kitchen to fix them their routine pot of tea after a meal.

"So, do you have any more information on the case?" she asked. "I'd like to get my head thinking about how I might put this book together."

"Actually, yeah," Charles said. "I can tell you how Dean was found. Officer Chase said it looked like a picture in a movie."

"Oh yeah?"

"Yeah, the door was broken, as you know," he explained. "And Dean's body was apparently slumped over onto his desk, his head resting right on the diary that Chief Mathers was reading from at the reception."

"That does sound rather like a movie scene," she agreed.

"But wait, that's not even the really weird part," he said. "Despite the door being broken, there were no signs of a struggle.

"So, let me get this straight. Someone broke down the door, and not only did Dean not fight back, but he unlocked the safe for his murderer?"

"I don't know if we can say for sure what happened until we have some more information, but it looks that way, yes," Charles answered.

Avery poured the tea and wondered how such a bizarre crime could take place. Charles was right in saying it was strange. There would have been an initial force, and then afterward, everything would have seemingly been quite easy for the murderer.

"So, how exactly was he murdered?" she asked.

Charles shrugged. "At the moment, the working theory is that it was suffocation. There are no visible markings on the body that officers would usually look for."

"And how common is it for someone to use suffocation as a murder tactic?" she asked.

"Not that common, but also not uncommon," he said. "It's not easy to do, that's the thing. It requires some strength, and usually, the victim puts up a struggle. But not in this case."

Avery sighed. "This is getting stranger with every word."

"If it wasn't for the broken door and the missing money, we would have just chalked it up to natural causes, most likely," Charles added.

"How can you be certain there was any money in the safe anyway?" she asked.

"Well, there had been a piece of paper in the safe with a record of what had been placed there and how much money it was," Charles explained. "Also, anybody that knew him knew he liked to travel with the same leather satchel. The police searched everywhere and could not find that satchel."

"Okay, so we have suffocation and missing money," Avery said. "That's not a lot to work with."

"Well, we think it was suffocation," Charles said. "There is no official cause of death yet. They're waiting for the autopsy results to come back."

"And you?" she asked. "Have they asked you to consult with them on the case?"

Charles flashed a cheeky smirk. "They have, but I don't think they need me," he said. "I think they want me to keep an eye on you."

Avery rolled her eyes as Charles cackled. It wasn't entirely impossible, given what had happened with previous investigations.

So much time was spent helping James solve pretend mysteries. How could I not get involved in a real one when it comes along?

"So how long until the cause of death is official?" she asked.

"A few days at max," Charles answered. "And it's tricky to investigate too much until then. A cause of death can dramatically change an investigation like this. But we can't exactly sit around and wait, either. People want to go home."

"Yes, I've had a couple of disgruntled guests," Avery said. "It seems, even in death, there are few people who care about Mr. Scott."

"It's a grim thought," Charles said. "But I suppose if you treat people badly as often as he did, these things happen."

"This is nothing like in the books that James wrote," Avery said. "By now, there would have been at least one foot chase and almost a high-speed car chase. Or at least a murder weapon."

"Yes, I suppose you might have to sprinkle those things in here and there in your version of events," he said. "I don't expect either of those things to happen."

Avery poured them another cup of tea, and they sipped in silence for a moment. There weren't many people whom Avery could sit with in silence and still enjoy their company, but Charles was one of those people.

"You know, you didn't have to close the vineyard today," Charles said. "I'm sure it would have been perfectly acceptable to operate."

"It just doesn't feel right," she said. "I don't want to deal with all the people who will be asking questions or gawking through the windows of his room."

"Who's to say anybody would gawk?" he said.

"Wouldn't you?"

Charles thought about it before confirming. "I suppose I might try to take a look, yes."

"You see?" she said. "Besides, it feels a little disrespectful. I know nobody liked him, but he did die last night. It just doesn't feel right to open up the gates and let people come here and drink wine and party up a storm."

"When you put it that way, I suppose I understand," he said. "I'm not complaining, though. I've had a lovely day off from work."

Avery chuckled as she drank her tea. She wondered if she would even have had the energy to run the farm that day. She was so exhausted from the night before and the cleaning she was actually happy to have the day off too.

"You're kind for doing that," Charles complimented her. "Not a lot of business owners would make that kind of sacrifice. It speaks volumes, and I know the locals will see that kindness, and it will benefit your business in the long run."

Avery smiled kindly at him. He was right. In a town like that, when most of her business relied on tourism, it didn't hurt to think that perhaps her farm would get even more support from the locals during the quiet months.

"Thanks, Charles," she said softly. "You always find the right words to say."

"Well, they're not just there to make you feel better," he said sternly. "They're the truth."

His words silenced her, if only for a moment, before a message on her phone reminded her of something that was bothering her tremendously. Avery frowned. "I'm sorry to change the subject, but I just don't think Deb did this. I know she was angry at him, and I know my word doesn't clear her name, but she just doesn't seem to fit the bill for this kind of murder. When a scorned woman commits murder, it's messy and violent. This doesn't fit that description."

"I agree with you there," Charles said. "It doesn't clear her name, but you're right. This doesn't look like the work of an angry ex-girlfriend."

"So, what kind of person would commit this kind of stranger murder?" she asked.

"You're asking all the right questions," Charles said. "And I am sure we are still going to learn a lot of shocking information about Mr. Scott. But as for now, my main suspect is a lot closer to him. I think it was Mrs. Scott."

Chapter Six

"Do you really think it could have been Mrs. Scott?" Avery asked as she placed her cup down neatly in the saucer. "I just can't imagine any mother murdering their own son."

"And yet, it happens all the time," Charles said. "News reports from all over the world have no shortage of murderous mothers."

"I suppose," Avery said, uncomfortable with the grim reality of it. "I guess I don't know Mrs. Scott at all. I've only ever seen her around in her all-white outfits. She seems like a demanding woman, but I don't know if she seems dangerous at all."

"Well, if you've never known her, you are lucky," he said. "You think Dean had a big ego? His mother's ego is at least twice as inflated. I don't think I've ever had a conversation with her where she hasn't spoken only about herself."

Avery had known someone like that before. It was tedious to have conversations like that, and she could picture Mrs. Scott being that way. It was something in the way she carried herself that made it easy to believe. She was an elderly woman but a fabulous one at that. Avery had never seen her without high heels on, and she knew how to control a room when she entered. It was an admirable trait, to say the least.

"Why do you see her as a suspect, Charles?" she asked. "It can't just be her inflated ego."

"It's a little more than that, yes," Charles said. "She's picked many fights in our community, and most of them she has won. And she's never won them fairly. She's the kind of woman who is quick to get the lawyers involved and will always get what she wants."

"I see," Avery said. "That is a quick way to make enemies, yes."

"Not only that but she's been on bad terms with Dean for months now," he continued. "Of course, she still loved him; I don't doubt that. But there were weeks when they didn't speak at all. She would go around telling everyone what a terrible son he was and how he didn't deserve anything she had ever given him."

"She is wealthy, I assume?" Avery asked.

"Oh, very."

"Then why did Dean steal all that money from Deb?" she asked again.

Charles shrugged. "From what I understand, he did it because he felt he deserved to spend that money. He really did think so highly of himself that he believed Deb owed him for the status he had given her while they were in a relationship."

"Now, that is egotistical," Avery said with wide eyes.

"He comes from generational wealth," Charles said. "And when Deb asked his family to pay off the debts he had created, they refused, saying she had embarrassed their family name by going to the police first."

Avery burst out laughing. "That's absurd! I can't believe what I'm hearing."

"Yes, that rose farm has been in the Scott family going back many generations," Charles explained. "But despite its success, it never gave Mrs. Scott the fame she longed for. Then, one year Mrs. Scott found a small amount of success when she won a beauty pageant. Through that, she was able to advertise the roses."

"She was a beauty queen?" Avery asked.

"Oh yes, and she won a lot of pageants after that, too," he said. "With her publicity, the rose farm boomed. They had always been wealthier than most, but after that, they secured enough money to last them many more generations."

Avery sipped her tea. "That must be nice," she said, thinking about her own farm.

"Yes," Charles said. "But Mrs. Scott soon started to see herself as some kind of small-town celebrity. She claims that she single-handedly put this place on the map."

"Sure," Avery said sarcastically. "It's got nothing to do with the world-renowned wines."

"The problem is that everybody started to treat her like a celebrity," Charles said. "And at first, they were just being polite and celebrating her success. But after a while, she started to expect it."

Avery imagined a young Mrs. Scott walking through the town, demanding free products as her photograph was taken. She wondered if she was ever asked to sign autographs. Avery had always felt fame would be a tedious, tiresome burden. She couldn't stand the thought of people constantly taking her photograph.

"She's a feisty woman, Mrs. Scott," Charles said. "And eventually, people were too afraid not to treat her like royalty. She is known to throw major fits if she doesn't get her way. People treat her well not out of respect but out of fear, and she doesn't seem to understand the difference."

"Surely not everybody is afraid of her?" Avery asked. "There has to be at least one person who is brave enough to stand up to her."

"I suppose she has a few close friends from before she was a pageant queen," Charles said softly. "But once, a coffee shop got her order wrong, and she went to the newspaper asking for them to be boycotted. It was ridiculous, and nobody followed her, of course. But it certainly made people afraid to upset her."

Avery laughed out loud. "Do you think I could get away with that?" she asked. "Do you think I could march through town and just demand that everybody treat me better? Maybe if I'm rude enough, or cause a big enough scene, then I can be treated like a celebrity, too."

Charles sunk his head into his hands. "Please don't ever do that," he begged. "It would be far too embarrassing. And I might change my opinion of you, then."

"I don't want that," Avery teased. "It's alright; I'm perfectly happy being treated like any old ordinary pleb."

"Me too," he agreed. "Being a drama queen sounds like hard work to me."

Avery smiled as she pictured Charles in large sunglasses, marching into the local news agency to report bad service at a nearby coffee shop. Then, she scribbled the thought down to add it to her book. She wouldn't tell Charles about it; she'd simply let him read it and laugh as she watched his face while he did.

The teapot was empty, and Avery carried it to the sink, where she ran a basin of soapy water. She and Charles had formed a routine after their meals. He had been visiting so often that he knew where everything was kept.

So, Avery would wash everything up, and Charles would dry each item and carefully pack it away. Usually, by the time

Charles left, there was no evidence of any food having been cooked or consumed in her kitchen. And she liked it that way.

They were about halfway through the dishes when they heard the sound of the candlesticks falling against the wooden table. And a few seconds later, Sprinkles entered the kitchen with the tablecloth hanging from his mouth.

"I guess he just wanted to help with the cleanup," Charles laughed as he took the cloth from the mouth of a very proud Sprinkles.

"I tell you, that dog training is great," Avery said. "But every so often, she teaches him a trick that I could live without."

"I think it's sweet," Charles said. "I'm just glad there weren't any plates left on there."

Charles disappeared to put the tablecloth back on the table as Avery continued to clean the dishes. She thought about everything Charles had told her about Mrs. Scott and pieced together a character description for her book.

"What had Dean and his mother been fighting about?" she asked when Charles returned. "You said they hadn't spoken in weeks."

"It was a major drama," Charles said. "Dean wanted his mother to move to the city and live with him. He said she was getting too old to run the farm, which, as I'm sure you can imagine, is the worst thing a pageant queen like her could hear."

Avery chuckled. "It's not something that any woman wants to hear...pageant queen or not."

"I suppose," Charles said with a laugh. "If I remember correctly, Dean had told his mother he wanted to sell the farm. He wanted the money and told her that if she didn't want to live with him he could put her into the fanciest old age home he could find."

Avery gasped. "No mother wants to hear that from their child. No wonder she was so angry with him."

"Well, it's no secret that Dean always hated the idea of inheriting the farm," Charles explained. "There was a time when he begged his mother to give him a sibling so the sibling could be the one faced with the task of running the farm after her death."

"He didn't want the family business?" Avery asked.

"No, he said that small-town living wasn't for him and nobody could ever make him change his mind. A couple of months ago, she was telling the local butcher he had already received a few offers for the farm, with the business included."

"I've driven past that farm," Avery said. "It's gorgeous. There are roses as far as the eye can see. It looks like something out of a fairytale."

"I know, so you can imagine that when Dean said he wanted to sell it, his mother kicked up a huge fuss," Charles said. "They fought about it for months. In fact, Deb said she heard them fighting at the coffee shop about it on the morning of the wedding, just a few hours before he died."

"That doesn't sound good," Avery said. "I understand why you see her as a suspect. But why would Dean want to sell a business that's been in his family for so long? Why not just keep it and let somebody else do the work for him?"

"You're asking the same question I am," Charles said. "So, I've suggested that one of the officers look into it. I'm not sure how or when they'll get any information on it. But, I suppose we'll have to find out one way or another."

"Why can't someone just ask her about it?"

"She just lost her son," Charles shrugged. "And she's a diva. When the officers did their initial questioning, it took them hours. She kept running out to lock herself in the bathroom to sob loudly. She even threatened to take legal action against the officer if he didn't solve the case by midnight."

"I see," Avery said. "That does seem dramatic."

"All I know is that she refuses to leave her farm and refuses to sell her business," Charles said. "And her inheritance states that she had no choice but to leave the farm to her nearest next of kin when she dies. She can't change it and leave it to someone else. Well...I suppose now that Dean's dead, she can."

"That's a grim thought, isn't it?" Avery quietly said as she washed the last of the dirty dishes.

"I suppose," Charles said. "There was a moment a few months ago where she had even said she would take legal action against her own son. It made me sad to think of it. Could a mother really feel that the land she owned was worth more than her relationship with her own son?"

"Well, they don't seem to respect each other the way a normal family would if you ask me," Avery said. "So, is it really all that surprising?"

Avery and Charles said goodbye to each other, and she watched as Sprinkles chased his car down the dirt road. She looked at the end of her property, where her parents lived in a small cottage, and breathed a sigh of relief, knowing that her family wasn't like Dean's.

She shuddered to imagine treating her parents the way Dean and his mother treated each other. Charles was right to look at Mrs. Scott as a suspect. She was a woman who would stop at nothing to get what she wanted, and women like that could be more volatile than most people.

Avery went back in and sat at the table where her notebook was and wrote countless notes and character traits. It was something she had seen James do at the start of every book. Afterward, she sat back and read through her notes again, making changes where she saw fit. Then she wrote down the description of the murder scene. There was something so interesting about it. It would have been a violent act to break the door down, yet other parts of the scene seemed so peaceful.

From Charles' information, she knew there were no signs of struggle. That meant he had no bruising or scratch marks and that there wasn't any blood. His body would have been in perfect condition, other than his non-beating heart.

Then there was the final detail of his head resting on the very thing that had been the largest clue to his investigation. Avery did her best not to, but before she knew it, she found herself walking softly across the lawn toward his room.

There was yellow police tape across the door, and she knew she could not go inside. Instead, she did the very thing she was worried her customers would do. She peered through the window.

Apart from the fingerprinting dust and the debris from the broken door, the room was in pristine condition. The cupboard door was open, and she could see the safe inside. It was entirely empty. The chair stood at the desk as if he had been sitting in it only moments ago. She wrote down what she needed to remember the scene and made her way back to the house.

Chapter Seven

A very was still full from her lunch with Charles when she arrived at the home of Eleanor and Samuel for tea. The sun would set in an hour or two, and she was already eager to climb into bed. She had enough notes to start creating some ideas for her book, and she wanted to work on them while it was still fresh in her mind.

The newlyweds welcomed her in and guided her through a sea of gift bags and boxes toward the patio. Their entire living room was drowning in wedding gifts, and Avery was certain it would take weeks for them to get through it all.

Every surface had another pile of gifts on it. All of them were still wrapped. Avery wondered what kind of gifts could be inside. It was always tough buying gifts for people who were already so well-established.

"I don't even want to know what's in half of these boxes," Eleanor said. "I'm at an age where I already have everything I want. I can't think what I might do with all of this."

Avery thought about it as if she were in Eleanor's shoes, and her hands became clammy from the stress. Eleanor was right. When you're more established in life, there is little need for that many wedding gifts.

"You'll have to put a shed in the back to store it all," Samuel teased. Eleanor shot him a glare.

It wasn't only the gifts. Samuel had moved in, so everywhere they walked, there was a chair or another item of furniture that hadn't found a home yet. There were still boxes to unpack, and according to Avery, it was a pretty chaotic way to start a marriage.

Outside was a lot calmer, and they couldn't even see the boxes from where they were sitting anymore. There were small cakes, pastries, and biscuits already waiting, and although Avery was full, she knew she could make space for at least some of the treats.

"We've had to postpone our honeymoon because of this murder," Eleanor said. "We should have been sipping sangria in Spain today."

"I'm sorry," Avery said, apologizing for something that was not her fault. "It's a terrible thing to have happened at a wedding. I'm sure the police could have timed it better, but what do I know about being a police officer?"

Avery knew Charles, but there hadn't been too many times that they'd talked about his career as a police officer. They talked about cases, sure, but never the finer details about what the job was actually like.

She hadn't seen Eleanor that upset before and wasn't sure how to react to it. Samuel didn't look too pleased either.

"He wasn't even invited," Samuel said. "Mrs. Scott gifted us with half the flowers for free, then after we accepted, insisted she bring a guest with her. With all those free flowers, we couldn't exactly say no, could we?"

"I suppose not," Avery said. "Did you know it was Dean that she was bringing, though?"

Eleanor shook her head. "She wouldn't tell us. She just said it was a surprise and that we'd all be pleased to see who it was. I had my suspicions, though."

"It seems completely insane to me that she'd do that," Samuel said. "From what I understand, it was common knowledge that nobody wanted to see him. And she knew Deb would be there."

"I see," Avery responded. "I didn't realize she'd sponsored half the flowers. Do you think she did that so you'd have no choice but to allow her to bring a guest?"

"Absolutely," Eleanor said. "I should have known Dean would throw a fit for not being invited. And it's just like him to do something like this, too."

Eleanor folded her arms as Samuel poured them each a cup of tea.

"Something like what?" Avery asked as she tried not to giggle at Eleanor's dramatic behavior.

"Trust Dean to be the center of attention always. He can't stand it when someone else has more eyes than he does," Eleanor said. "So, trust him to go and get himself murdered on the day of my wedding."

Avery had known narcissists before, and most of them had a stubborn determination to survive. The ones she had known had felt so important that the concept of dying seemed to be a detriment that was only a danger to those lesser than them.

"I don't think he arranged his own murder," Avery said. "That's not exactly something one does out of spite."

"No, I suppose you're right," Eleanor said, relaxing her shoulders. "And we're very happy to be married. It's just...that thing he wrote in his diary has me annoyed."

"How so?"

"He makes it seem as if we're all against him, but he put

himself in that position," she explained. "If he had just treated everyone with respect, he might have been more accepted in this community."

"As far as I can tell, he was quite the narcissist, so I wouldn't take it too personally if I were you," Avery said with a smile. "What happened with your honeymoon, by the way?"

At that point, Samuel started to show some signs of frustration. "We've had to postpone it, obviously," he said. "The police said we can't go anywhere. It's so ridiculous if you ask me."

"They've insisted they see all the film footage of the day, too," Eleanor added. "We haven't even been able to see a single snippet or photograph yet."

"I'm sorry to hear about that," Avery said, reaching for another treat. "But I'm happy to hear you were able to postpone the honeymoon."

"Only by a few days," Samuel explained. "It's a bit concerning, to be honest. We were only able to push it slightly forward on account of the resort being fully booked. And we've already paid, so we couldn't just find a new resort."

"We're worried that this won't be sorted out in time," Eleanor said. "It's a beautiful honeymoon that we've booked. But the police won't give us any information on how long this might take. It's all too stressful."

Avery felt bad for them. She could see how tense they were about the subject. She could only imagine after months of planning and preparation and a murder at their wedding, they were more than eager to jet off to Spain and leave it all behind for a while.

"Surely you have been cleared as suspects, though?" she asked. "I mean, they can't possibly think that the bride or groom would leave their own wedding to commit this murder."

Samuel sighed. "Of course, they don't see us as suspects. But they have told us to stay behind in case they have further questions for us or need anything more from us. You know, since it was our wedding he was attending and since they think it was one of our guests."

"Even in death, he's managed to ruin the fun for all of us," Eleanor said, biting her nail. "I have half a mind to show up at Mrs. Scott's house and give her a piece of my mind for bringing him along at all."

Samuel placed a comforting hand on Eleanor's leg and smiled. "I'm sure everything will work out fine, my love," he said.

"I know, I know," Eleanor said, taking a deep breath. "It's just that we have so much to lose if we don't make it to this honeymoon."

"Like what?" Avery asked without thinking. She realized after she had asked the question that it was probably none of her business. But the question had sort of just slipped out. Watching the two of them get riled up over the murder was like watching a soap opera. There was drama, emotion, and romance involved. It reminded her of the shows she used to watch when she was much younger.

"Well, our honeymoon is non-refundable," Samuel said. "It was all part of a package. So, if we can't make the new dates that we've arranged, we will lose every last cent we have paid toward it."

Avery had been more involved in the wedding planning than she had liked. The entire Stammtisch had helped Eleanor put it together. It meant that Avery had a vague idea of how much the wedding had cost, and the idea of them losing the honeymoon money made her feel ill. It wasn't her money, and she knew well enough that none of that stress was of her concern. But she cared about Eleanor and Samuel, which meant that inevitably, if they were stressed, then so was she.

She wondered if Deb or Camille felt the stress of others, too. Deb knew just about everybody, and Avery shuddered to think of how much stress she would feel if she was like Avery and also took on her friend's stresses.

"Yes," Eleanor said, bringing Avery's attention back to the conversation. "If this doesn't work out, then Dean will have not only managed to ruin my wedding but also our honeymoon. After everything we've had to pay for, it will be a long time before we can afford a holiday again."

"Well, I don't want to think about that," Samuel said. "Because I think it will all work out fine."

"Sorry, Avery," Eleanor said. "You're our first visitor since the wedding, so we're kind of piling it all on you here, aren't we?"

Eleanor dropped her shoulders and looked genuinely upset about the conversation. It made Avery feel a bit better. She felt bad for Eleanor and knew how important it was to talk to others when things that were planned perfectly go completely awry.

Avery laughed. "Don't worry. That's what friends are for. Besides, you guys can keep talking, and I'll just keep eating."

Avery reached for another macaron of a different flavor this time. She didn't have the capacity to eat it, but it looked so delicious that she bit into it anyway. Her desire had overrun her logic, and she knew she would pay for it when her stomach was so full that she could barely move later. But as she bit into it, any potential regret she once felt simply melted away.

"How are you doing?" Samuel asked. "I believe you've closed the farm today."

"Yes," Avery said. "It just didn't feel right to carry on so soon after everything happened. But other than that, I'm alright."

Avery took a sip of tea, washing down the sugary frosting from a piece of cake. "Actually," she continued. "The police have agreed to let me follow them on the case, and then I can write a book inspired by it afterward."

"Oh, that's fun!" Eleanor said. "You must be so excited. I can't wait to read it."

"Yes," Samuel laughed. "And I'm sure this case is bound to take a few turns, given how little information is available at the moment."

"So, do you have some inside information for us?" Eleanor asked. "Does it look like we'll make it to our honeymoon?" Eleanor looked longingly at her, and for the first time since they had sat down, her leg stopped twitching. She dropped her hands into her lap and waited for the answer she was hoping to hear.

But Avery couldn't give it to her. Avery shrugged. "I don't have much, and it is hard to say," she said. "But I promise you they are putting all the energy possible into solving this."

"You see, honey?" Samuel said. "They're going to get this sorted in no time, and we'll fly off to Spain and simply forget about it all."

Eleanor gave him a relieved smile. "I guess you're right, as always," she said.

"By the way," Avery said. "Just out of curiosity...who do you think did it?"

"You mean, who committed the murder?" Samuel asked with wide eyes. Avery nodded as she sipped her tea.

"It's hard to say," Eleanor answered. "A lot of people

hated his guts. But I don't know if anyone hated him enough to murder him. Murder just seems like a lot of effort to put into someone you hate."

She had a point. Avery hadn't thought about it that way. Even some crimes of passion weren't born out of hate but out of extreme love. Surely, if anyone hated him that much, they would rather just avoid him.

But the missing money made it seem so planned out and so thought out. "Who would know about the money?" Avery asked. "You know, the bag that was stolen."

Eleanor rolled her eyes. "Anybody that knew him, to be honest. He had a habit of bragging with his cash."

Samuel burst out laughing. "Yes, I only ever met him once, and he even showed it to me. It did strike me as rather odd."

Avery agreed with Samuel. That was an odd thing to do, but the man clearly thought very highly of himself and seemed to have desperately needed to show everyone how important and successful he was.

"And poor Deb," Eleanor added. "They questioned her for hours. And everyone knows it couldn't have been her."

"Yes," Samuel agreed. "She doesn't quite strike me as the murdering type."

The three of them enjoyed their tea as Avery diverted the conversation elsewhere. She could see that it was eating at them and hoped she could create some kind of brief distraction for them. She wondered if that hadn't been why she'd been invited there in the first place.

"Well, let me not keep you two much longer," Avery said, sipping the last of her tea.

The sun was starting to set rapidly, and she knew that after the morning of cleaning and the late night the night before, it wouldn't take her too long to fall asleep. And she was eager for sleep too. Already her eyes burned, and her eyelids felt heavy, and with a belly full of decadent treats, she knew she'd be fast asleep soon enough.

She said goodbye to her friends as she left their driveway. When she glanced back at them, she could see how tired and stressed they were. It showed in the bags underneath their eyes and the slump in their shoulders.

As she drove, Avery thought about the information she already had. She had hoped that the question about the money would narrow down the search. But learning he was the kind of man to show off that type of thing, she felt like it had the opposite effect.

It could have been anyone. The only people Avery knew it certainly couldn't have been were the people who were still present when the police had stopped the music. But by then, many people had already left the party.

Avery knew they needed to move quickly and wondered what she could do to speed things up. She hated the thought of the newlyweds not being able to go on their honeymoon because of a man nobody liked that hadn't even been invited.

Chapter Eight

Avery stood in front of the bookstore and smiled. She had visited that store since she was a child, and it was still her favorite place in the town. It was two stories of secondhand books, and to someone like Avery, it might as well have been a building filled with treasure.

It was an older building with wooden doors and window frames. There were a few steps inside covered in sandstone. A metal spiral staircase led to the upper floor. There were rows of bookshelves against every wall, and in the center of every room, a table with piles of books on top.

She wondered how many hours of her life she had already spent there. It had never changed. The same family had owned the business for as long as she could remember, and even the cash register was still the same.

The bookstore was the only place Avery ever spent her pocket money growing up.

Thankfully, a small coffee shop had opened right next door. So, Avery stopped there and ordered two coffees to go. It was early morning, and the bookstore had only just opened.

Already, there were a fair amount of people inside. The

bookstore had made a name for itself and was one of the tourist destinations in the town. Avery was expecting to meet Charles and her father there for some browsing.

She wasn't ready to open the vineyard up to guests yet and was desperate to find new books to read. James had always told her that nobody could ever expect to be a decent writer if they weren't reading decent books. So, Avery planned on stocking up on all the best books she could find. She had a book that she wanted to write, and she intended to write it well. And it was never a bad idea to fill up on inspiration with every opportunity.

Avery stepped inside, coffee in each hand and Sprinkles following closely behind her. She couldn't reach out and take any books yet because of the coffees, but she could at least read the titles and narrow down her potential selection.

She stared at the first shelf for almost five minutes, just reading over the titles and admiring the artwork on the spines. She wondered what her book might look like once it was done and ready to publish.

She imagined that maybe one day she might walk into that bookstore and find her own book on the shelf and hoped that it would have a particularly bent and used spine. The worse the condition was, the more it had been read. She had learned that as a kid. Since then, she'd gravitated to books that looked in bad shape. The more folds and bends it had in the spine, the more times it had been opened. It was a really good book if she opened it and found that some of the pages had been taped back together. A person only goes through that much effort if you intend to read the book again and again. And the best part was that the damaged books were usually cheaper too.

She inhaled and enjoyed the smell of the bookstore, the scent of old pages and wooden bookshelves. She remembered how she used to imagine living in a home that looked just like it one day. And for a while, she did. When she lived with James, they had rows and rows of books. She hadn't had the heart to unpack any of them yet. They lived in boxes.

The thought of all her books living in boxes made her sad, but she was quickly distracted when she noticed Sprinkles was no longer sitting politely at her ankles. Then, she heard a familiar whining sound. She looked over to the cash register and saw Sprinkles whining at the counter. Simon, the current owner of the shop, tried to pat Sprinkles, but he moved away.

"So sorry, Simon," Avery said as she tried to pull Sprinkles away from the counter.

"It's no problem!" Simon said with a friendly smile. "I suppose he's just after one of my snacks." Simon lifted a sandwich out from behind the counter and chuckled. "It's an odd breakfast, I know," he said. "But I do love a decent sandwich."

"There's nothing wrong with a sandwich for breakfast!" Avery laughed as she tried some more to get Sprinkles to leave him alone. However, she much preferred the breakfast of a puffy pancake, like the one she'd had that morning, to a sandwich.

But Sprinkles sat dead still and wouldn't move. He whined some more with his eyes fixated on the counter in front of him. Avery thought it odd. It had been some time since Sprinkles had begged. She wondered what might be on that sandwich that could smell so delicious that Sprinkles would forget his manners entirely. Eventually, she gave up, and Simon assured her that Sprinkles was no bother at all.

At that moment, Charles finally arrived a few minutes late. "Here," she said, shoving the coffee in his hands.

"Oh!" he said with a smile. "How did you know I needed one?"

"It's before noon," Avery laughed. "You need multiple coffees before noon."

"It's true!" he said, eagerly taking a sip.

The two of them walked through the first shelves.

"I hope you don't mind that I've invited my father along," Avery said. "When he heard we were coming to the bookstore, he insisted on joining us. He loves this place just as much as I do."

"It really is no trouble," Charles said. "I thought he'd be coming with you, though?"

Avery laughed. "No, my father's getting old, and so he is determined to prove he is still capable. He refused to let me drive him!" Charles laughed so hard he nearly choked on his coffee. "He offered to give me a lift," Avery giggled. "But I've seen how he drives these days, and I was too terrified. So, I told him I had other errands to run after this."

Charles and Avery shared a chuckle as she reached for a tattered book on the shelf in front of her. But she couldn't concentrate on the blurb on the back because she could still hear Sprinkles whining. She put the book back and reached into her bag for his lead.

"Sorry, Simon," she said again. "Let me get him out of your hair." She clipped the lead onto his harness and gave a soft tug. Sprinkles obliged and left Simon alone.

"I don't even have any sandwich left!" Simon laughed. "And still, he wants a bite!"

Avery let out a weak chuckle and hooked the loop of the lead over her arm. Sprinkles was good with his lead and required little convincing to follow her around. She returned to the book she was looking at and opened it up.

She saw some pencil lines underlining sentences that must have been of some importance to the previous owner. She immediately knew she wanted to read the book and tucked it under her arm.

"Got something so soon?" Charles laughed. "We've hardly even been here."

"I know how to spot a good book," Avery said with a wink. "Besides, I never leave here without a fair stack."

Avery and Sprinkles followed Charles upstairs to the upper floor. There wasn't much room upstairs, but thankfully, they were the only two up there. Avery led Sprinkles to one corner of the room and told him to stay there. And he happily obliged. He lay down comfortably and watched as she and Charles browsed the section with of cookbooks.

"I wonder what will happen to this place now that Dean has died," Charles commented.

"What do you mean?"

"Well, this building belonged to him," Charles said. "It's been in his family some time, and for his thirtieth birthday, his mother officially signed it over to him as a birthday gift."

"That's quite a gift," Avery commented.

"Indeed," Charles chuckled. "The best gift my family ever got me was a bicycle."

Avery ran her fingers along the spines of the books as she waited to find one that was damaged enough for her to inspect. She also kept a close eye on the kinds of books Charles was pulling from the shelves. She was curious to know what occupied his mind when he was spending his nights at home.

"I don't understand," Avery said. "Surely then the building will just go back to his mother? Why would his death affect the bookstore?"

"Didn't you hear?" Charles asked as he pulled a sci-fi book from the shelf. "Dean was going to sell the building to some developer to turn into a hotel."

"A hotel?" Avery laughed. "Instead of the bookstore? I could never imagine such a thing!"

"Yes, I know," Charles sighed. "It does seem ridiculous. Never mind the idea of a full hotel all the way out here. This isn't exactly a hotel kind of place, is it?"

"Well, I have a guest house," Avery reminded him.

"Yes, well, that's different," Charles said. "That still fits in here. A hotel with valets and room service and all that city stuff makes no sense to me out here."

"I suppose," Avery sighed. "Simon must have been devastated when he heard the news."

"That's an understatement," Charles said. "I believe he phoned up a lawyer the moment he heard about it. Not sure what he planned on doing. I mean, the owner of a building can do what he wants with it."

"But this place has always been here," Avery said. "For as long as I can remember. It can't move. It won't be the same."

"Well, a lot of people feel that way," he said. "There was quite an uproar."

"So what do you think will happen to the store?" Avery asked.

"I'm not sure," Charles said. "But I tell you, the timing of his death is pretty good. The sale was meant to go through in a couple of weeks."

"Do you think his mother would go through with the sale?" she asked.

Charles shook his head. "She was against the idea entirely. She's a sentimental woman, you see. It's a family heirloom, this place. She wants it to stay in the family."

"So the bookstore won't close?" Avery said with a forced pout.

"I don't think so," Charles answered. "Not anymore."

Avery breathed a quiet sigh of relief. For as long as she

could remember, she would escape to that bookstore any time she needed to find some peace. She didn't know what she would do if it closed. And she thought of Simon and how upset he would have been. She thought of his family and how long they had worked in the building. Without that space, their business would never be the same again.

Then it hit her—what Charles was really saying. She marched up to him and spoke as quietly as she could. "Charles, you don't think Simon is a suspect, do you?"

"He might be," Charles answered quietly. "He was at the wedding, and he has a decent motive. He stands to gain from Dean's death, doesn't he?"

"I suppose," she said as her heart dropped into the soles of her shoes. She thought of all the lengths she might go to in order to protect her own business. She would do just about anything but didn't think she would kill anyone. Then again, she'd never experienced a threat like Simon had.

She knew enough about him to know how badly he needed the business. He had three kids and a wife. He was the sole earner for his family. He told her that once when she had been the only one in the store and they had started talking. He had a lot to lose if the deal had gone through.

"I don't believe it," Avery whispered.

"I hate to break it to you," Charles said. "But when we solve this, I don't think any of us are going to like the truth. Someone at that wedding did it. It's bound to be someone we know personally on some level."

Chapter Nine

Avery recognized her father's voice as he loudly greeted Simon downstairs. Avery and Charles made their way to him. He had reached an age where he refused to believe he was going deaf, so every word out of his mouth was too loud for normal conversation.

"Morning, Dad," she said, giving him a hug. "I hope you don't mind that I didn't get you a coffee."

"That's for the best," he said with a smile. "I can't drink coffee anymore. It goes right through me."

Charles laughed as he said good morning to her father, and they resumed their browsing. But Avery kept glancing at Simon, who seemed to be invested in whichever book he was reading. She looked at him and tried to picture him breaking the door down to murder Dean. It just didn't suit him. He was so friendly and calm. She couldn't imagine that amount of violence or hatred coming from him.

But murderers hardly ever look like murderers.

Sprinkles loved her father, so with his lead in his mouth, he trudged along after him throughout the store. His nose was always pointed up at him, and his eyes glistened like stars whenever her father was around. His tail wagged, kicking up dust from the hardwood floors and making a light knocking sound with every beat. The reason for that was Avery's father had a habit of carrying dog treats in his pocket that he would sneak to Sprinkles when he thought nobody was watching. Of course, in his old age, he wasn't as sneaky as he thought he was, and Avery had caught him almost every time.

Avery glanced up and saw the name *James Parker* printed on a spine in front of her. She almost gasped out loud when she saw it. It had been so long since she'd seen one of her husband's books on a shelf. And there were rows of them, with most of them in bad shape. She smiled a little as she looked at them all. It made her miss him. She hadn't ever seen his book with a bent spine. She had been there when he had written them, so they had always already known the book well enough by the time they were sent to print. All the copies she had were in pristine condition. They had never been opened. They looked better with some wear and tear, though. It was a far more appealing look. Each book used the same font, and the spines were various colors. She remembered how much time he would spend choosing each color to make sure it worked with the story.

She reached for one of the books where her husband had modeled the main character after her. She looked it over and saw it had all the markers she would usually look for in a book. The spine was so bent that it was almost falling apart. There were scuff marks all along the edges. And when she looked inside, she found that some of the pages had been taped back together. She wondered if there was a name for who it had belonged to in the front of the book.

She flipped to the first page and found a handwritten note scribbled in red ink.

Darling,

May this be a teaser for an already perfect mind. You can read this on our holiday, with your feet in the warm white sand.

I love you.

Your ever-devoted husband.

At that moment, she felt no sadness anymore. Of course, she still missed her husband, but she could see the effect that his life had on others. She knew she was not the only person missing him. He had a following of readers who likely missed him too. And it made her feel a little less alone.

"Come have a look here, Avery," her father called out way too loudly.

He had some arbitrary book about accounting in the middle ages in hand, and she knew that he was simply trying to distract her from the shelf in front of her. Still, she tucked her husband's book under her arm. She would take it home and put it on her shelf so she could remember him the way his readers did. Then she walked with her father as he browsed the military section.

"You know, that Dean was a terrible man," he said.

"What made you think of that?" she asked with a laugh.

"I saw a book about cops, and it made me think of my friend Carl, which made me think of that guy Dean."

"Ah," Avery chuckled.

"My friend Carl lost his job because of Dean. Did you know that?" he asked.

"I didn't even know you had a friend named Carl," Avery said.

"Well, I do," her father snapped. "But I haven't seen him in a while. Thanks to that guy Dean."

Avery quickly looked around the bookstore to see who could hear them, but most of the other customers had left, and Simon didn't seem to be paying attention.

"Carl is a good man," her father explained. "He worked as a cop, and all he wanted to do was help people. And he was good at being a cop."

"So what happened?" Avery asked, motioning for Charles to take a step closer so he could also hear.

"Well, when Dean left Deb with all that debt, Carl felt that their attempts hadn't been good enough to help her," her father explained. "He decided that if Deb had paid for the furniture, it belonged to her."

"I tend to agree with that," Charles said.

"Because you're also a good cop," her father laughed. "So, Carl arrived at Dean's city house one day with the local sheriff there to repossess all the furniture."

Charles became a little uneasy. "Did he have the proper paperwork for that? It can't have been easy to arrange."

"No, but the cops on that side agreed with him, and so they made something happen," her father continued. "But they were barely through the door before Dean's lawyer arrived."

Her father picked out a book that was almost pristine and tucked it under his arm. Avery wanted to stop him and explain that it couldn't possibly be a good book, but he was mid-story and half deaf, so she knew it was no use.

"I don't know exactly how," her father continued as he waved his hands through the air. "But his lawyer knew some other fancy city lawyer."

"That's never good," Charles commented as he reached for a Japanese cooking book.

Avery did her best not to giggle as she envisioned Charles preparing sushi for them one afternoon. He wasn't much of a chef, and perhaps cookbooks weren't a bad idea for him to be buying. But Japanese recipes seemed to be a brave choice.

"No, it wasn't," her father snapped, bringing her attention back to the story. "That fancy lawyer man found some loophole or other and pressed charges against Carl. It was such a story, and the news even got involved."

"That's bound to lose you your job," Charles said, putting the cookbook down again.

"That's precisely what happened," her father explained. "They agreed to drop the charges if he was never employed as a police officer again. It made all of us so angry."

Avery understood why. Dean had done wrong, and Deb had to suffer. Carl was only trying to do the right thing and give Dean what he deserved. Dean, in turn, ruined his life, too.

"And I tell you, Carl never recovered from that," her father said. "He loved being a cop. It was all he ever wanted to do. I grew up with him, and since he was a kid, he was pretending to arrest people in the street with a gun-shaped twig."

"What did he do after losing his job?" Charles asked. Charles was no longer paying any attention to the books at all. He was completely invested in the story, and as a retired cop, Avery could understand why. Charles had left on his own terms, and even then, he continued to consult. People who become cops have a passion for correcting the wrongs in the world.

"He went down a bad path," her father explained. "He was depressed and couldn't seem to keep a job for very long. It was really sad to see him that way."

"I'm sorry to hear about that," Charles added. "I can't imagine what I would have done in that situation."

"That's not even the worst of it!" her father shouted. "His life only went downhill from there."

Her father reached for another book and took a pause in his story to first read the blurb before shaking his head and placing it back on the shelf.

"His wife couldn't take the stress anymore," her father continued with his story. "She took the kids and went to live with her family in another state. She had lost all faith in him as a husband. He never saw it coming."

"That's terrible," Avery whispered.

The story was worse than she ever could have imagined, and she wondered how Dean could have lived with himself for so many years, knowing how many lives he had ruined and how many lives he intended to ruin. And he did it for money.

"Carl never saw his kids again," her father explained. "He could never afford to go there to see them or to bring them down here for a visit. And with his wife and kids gone, he had nothing to work for. He no longer cared much for himself. So, his health took a turn for the worst."

"Where is he now?" Charles asked.

"Well, he lost his house, of course," her father said with a heavy sigh. "He couldn't afford to pay for it at all."

"Please don't tell me it gets worse than that," Avery said, desperate for the sad story to end.

Only it wasn't a sad story. It was someone's actual life that had been ruined by the victim. Carl wasn't some imaginary character in one of the books on the shelf. He was out there somewhere paying the price for trying to be a better cop.

"He eventually did get back on his feet a little," her father said. "Started to do some odd jobs here and there and found a place to live. But he never did see his kids again. Perhaps he still will one day."

"Carl is still alive?" Charles snapped.

"Of course!" her father answered. "He lives in a small cottage at the end of the Winston's property. They've given him a good deal there. He helps them out on the farm where they need it, and he gets to stay there."

"That's at least a bit of good news," Avery said.

"When I spoke to him last, he said he was saving some money to go see his children," her father said. "I hope he does. He's getting old now, like me, and I'd hate for him to die without ever having seen them again."

Then her father shrugged. "He will never recover from the debt of it all, though," he said. "And he blames it all on that Dean."

"He does?" Charles asked. "Has he said that to you?"

Her father raised his eyebrows. "Of course, he has! He's always telling me how much he hates the entire Scott family for how they treat their neighbors."

Avery looked at Charles and knew exactly what he was thinking. He excused himself and thanked them for the visit. She knew he was going to the police station to list Carl as a possible suspect. He had a decent motive, she knew. What's worse was that he had little to lose at that point in his life. Even to Avery, he seemed like a strong suspect in the murder. Her father had given them a clue without even knowing it.

Avery felt completely overwhelmed by the day, and it was still morning. She had woken up that morning with the intention of finding a new book to read, and instead, she discovered two new suspects in a murder case.

Chapter Ten

The Stammtisch women had gathered at Deb's house for a quick cup of coffee. They were eager to see each other after the wedding. The last few full gatherings of the group largely involved planning and preparation for the wedding, and this time there would be none of that, only some catching up.

"Sorry it couldn't be at my house," Eleanor said. "My home is still piled under unopened gifts. I just can't get myself to open any of them!"

"That's alright!" Deb said happily. "I'm always eager to host you all. You fill my home with laughter and cheer, and that is never a bad thing."

Deb had a fairly large home. It was minimalist and decorated with various shades of light gray. Even the coffee cups were gray, and so was Deb's outfit. The only bit of color Avery could see that wasn't part of their clothing came from the hot coffee in the cups.

The house was so pristine that Avery always had a hard time getting comfortable. She was constantly afraid she might move something out of place and that it might upset Deb. It felt like sitting in a show house.

"Did they treat you alright at the police station?" Eleanor asked with worry.

"Oh yes," Deb answered. "They gave me food and water and coffee, and I was allowed to go outside from time to time to stretch my legs. It's their slow online system that makes it all take so long. But they were friendly, so it wasn't too bad." Deb reached for her cup of coffee and took a sip. "The chairs are awfully uncomfortable, and everything in there is so boring. It was only a few hours, but I missed home."

Avery chuckled quietly at the irony of it. She wondered if the gray inside walls of the police station weren't perhaps similar to the inside of Deb's home.

"Have they cleared your name then?" Avery asked.

Deb rolled her eyes. "No, and I'm apparently not supposed to talk about any of this. But there is no chance I am keeping quiet," she answered. "Despite all of you being able to say you saw me at the wedding all night, they say they can't confidently agree that I didn't do it."

Eleanor shook her head and looked as if she might cry. It did not go unnoticed by Deb.

"At the end of the day, they have no evidence that I actually did do it," Deb continued. "All they have is a motive. But if you ask me, that makes half the town a suspect."

"I'm sorry to hear about that," Avery said quietly.

"Me too," Eleanor said bluntly. "Until they sort this out, there is a high chance I might lose my honeymoon. We still can't get the hotel to budge on our booking."

"That's terrible," Camille piped up with what would likely be her only words for the entire visit.

Deb and Camille had always gotten along very well, and it had always amused the rest of them. Deb could hardly ever stop talking, and Camille barely ever spoke. It seemed like a perfect match.

"Well, I think I might have something to cheer you up," Deb said to Eleanor. "I have a surprise for you!"

Deb leaned forward and grabbed the television remote, which was remarkably gray. She pointed it at her television, which was framed in a pale gray frame, and switched it on. Deb was bouncing in her seat with excitement.

"I have the first batch of footage from the wedding ready to show you," she said with a wide smile.

Deb's wedding gift to Eleanor was to be the videographer for the wedding. Avery had been upset when she heard of it. She wished she had thought about it. Then again, it was Deb that suggested Avery gift all the wine.

Deb pushed the play button, and the screen filled with scenes of all the guests dancing wildly to the music. "Now, I don't have all of it yet," Deb said. "But I do have the dance party, and there are some really great shots here that I wanted to show you."

The entire group burst out laughing when the image of Charles hugging the wine bottle filled the screen. It was even funnier than Avery had remembered, and she had to put her coffee down to avoid spilling all over Deb's light gray sofa.

Then the moment turned sweeter when the camera panned to Camille, her hands holding Sprinkles' front paws as they moved around slowly across the dance floor. And once again, Sprinkles stole the show.

Eleanor was smiling widely as she watched it. It was good to see her looking at her wedding with a smile. There had been nothing but stress for her since the wedding ended, and Avery was happy to know she was being reminded of how great the party had been.

By the time Avery left Deb's house, she felt relaxed. And

the coffee had done an excellent job of renewing her energy for Sprinkles' training class. He had already done well, and she had decided to keep doing the training for a while longer.

It was a bright and sunny day at the park where the training was happening, and Sprinkles had become part of a larger class. He no longer needed one-on-one lessons, as he was comfortable around other dogs. And it was good for him to socialize. Already, Avery knew which dogs he preferred to be around, and she even considered making friends with their owners.

That day, Sprinkles performed well in his class. He didn't make a single mistake and followed orders perfectly. She wondered why he had behaved so badly at the bookstore and wanted to know if she had been doing something wrong that day.

Then she thought about the day of the wedding when Sprinkles had sniffed Dean's hand. They had practiced that walk and return many times. Not once had Sprinkles veered from the path or stopped for anything. It was possible that the crowd had made Sprinkles less obedient. He'd always loved to be around people, and she had once or twice before struggled to get him to listen. But that was when he was a very small puppy.

He hadn't misbehaved for months before that day. Then, at the wedding and the bookstore, he suddenly seemed not to listen to her anymore.

But at training, he performed perfectly. He completed every trick without much persuasion needed. He did not beg for food or veer from his path, despite there being a small crowd of other dogs and owners.

It just simply made no sense to her. She couldn't think of anything she might have done differently, but she decided to speak to Brie, the dog trainer, and see what her opinion was.

By the time the training was over, Sprinkles was pretty tired. He collapsed at her feet with a wide smile and his tongue hanging out the side of his mouth. Avery petted him on the head as she refilled his water bowl.

"We'll go home soon enough," she said to Sprinkles. "I just need to ask your teacher something."

She searched for Brie, hoping to catch her and ask her why Sprinkles had not listened to her those two times, but Brie was already in conversation with another woman. Avery waited for a while, but it quickly became apparent that the conversation wouldn't be ending soon.

The woman was much older and had wrapped her hand around Brie's arm in a death grip. Avery knew that grip all too well. It was what elderly women did to stop you from leaving before they were done telling their stories.

Brie looked impatient about it, too. Of course, she was smiling and friendly, but every time she looked up in Avery's direction, her eyes sent out a cry for help. It made Avery laugh a little to see it. She wondered if she would ever be that way when she was older.

By the time Brie looked up for the third time, she thought Brie might be on the verge of crying. Avery wanted to do something to help, but as she glanced down at her watch, she realized that she was completely out of time.

She had promised Charles that she would cook dinner for him. The police had let her know that they no longer needed access to the room and it could be cleaned and reopened for business. Charles had kindly agreed to go in and do the cleaning up for her. He had also arranged for someone to fix the door. It had been am incredibly generous offer, and Avery didn't want to be late for him. So, she mouthed an apology to Brie and loaded Sprinkles in the car to head home. She felt awful leaving Brie in that situation, but she knew it would eventually end.

Sprinkles slept soundly as they drove. His face rested on his front paws, and he breathed loudly enough that Avery could hear it on the front seat. She put on his favorite classical music for him and made the short trip home.

When she arrived home, she looked over at the guest house and felt differently about it. She knew that if she went to Dean's room, it would likely look the way it had before he had ever stayed there. She saw a bin bag filled with yellow tape waiting to be taken away. She breathed a sigh of relief, knowing that the last reminders of what happened there were being removed. It had been tough for the guests who still had to stay in their rooms to walk past the yellow crime scene tape every day, and with that up, there was no chance of her booking out any more rooms.

As she parked the car, she ran through the list of suspects in her head. She wondered which one of them had enough strength to break down the door. Both Simon and Carl had a good enough motive. But did either of them have the strength required?

She didn't know Carl and didn't even know what he looked like. But she did know that he had been a cop once. It wasn't entirely impossible that he had remained in good shape even after he had lost his job.

Her mind was about to be distracted when she, thankfully, found something else to concentrate on. Avery's mind filled with the scent of fragrant herbs as she started preparing dinner for her and Charles. She was excited to cook his favorite childhood recipe of lasagna soup. Avery had been cooking for him regularly for so long that she knew what his favorite meal was, and she prepared it for him that night.

She wondered if other people also had friends who were

as good as hers. And as she cooked, all thoughts of the murder filtered out of her mind for a while. She simply moved effortlessly through the kitchen as she reached for ingredients.

Avery knew that cooking could help her process just about anything. It was what she had relied on after her husband had died, and it had given her peace since.

She loved it even more if she was cooking for somebody else. That was when she got really creative, serving up the best that she had to offer that day.

Just before the dinner was ready and Charles was set to arrive, she put on some music and opened a bottle of Le Blanc's aged cabernet sauvignon, leaving it on the table to aerate before their dinner began. It was one of Le Blanc Cellars' best bottles. Avery chuckled, thinking of her pairing this sophisticated cab sauv with Charles' simple but favorite meal. It was the least she could do to thank him; besides, Avery was always eager for a reason to enjoy the good stuff in life.

Chapter Eleven

The table was set outside on the patio. It was a perfect summer night, and soft lights came from the garden around them. Sprinkles slept deeply at their feet as Avery and Charles enjoyed their dinner together.

The food had turned out even better than she had expected. The music was still playing quietly inside, and Sprinkles took deep, calming breaths as he slept. It had been a good day for Avery, and she couldn't think of a better way to end it.

The vineyard was quiet, and the last of the birds chirped happily as they flew by on the way to their homes. The first light of the stars was speckling the sky.

Charles hadn't said a word in a few minutes. He had been too busy finishing his meal. That was normal if he enjoyed his food. It was as if all thoughts of the real world simply evaporated from his mind, and his sole focus became the food that he was eating. He and Sprinkles were oddly similar in that way.

The wine she had opened paired perfectly with their meal, and it was one of the most enjoyable evenings that Avery had

had in a long time. So, she ate as slowly as she could, savoring every moment of their dinner together.

It was a special thing to her to have a friendship so lovely that the two of them could be completely comfortable sitting in silence together. She knew the silence wouldn't last long, but still, it didn't make her feel uncomfortable.

When Charles finally ate the last bite of his food, he leaned back in his seat with his glass of wine in his hand. "So, what do we think about the suspects?" he asked. "If this was a book, and you were writing it, which you are...but if it wasn't real life, which one of our suspects would you choose to be the murderer?"

"I have to admit that both Carl and Simon have excellent motives," she answered. "And I was just wondering earlier which one of them might be strong enough to break down the door."

"You're thinking more like a cop every day," Charles said. "But those doors are surprisingly easy to break. It's an old cellar door. I don't think that should be too much of a focus."

"Oh," she answered, almost disappointed at the amount of thought energy she had wasted on that point in particular. "Well, we have one man who was going to lose his entire life's work if Dean wasn't stopped," Avery said. "And then we have another man who did lose his entire life's work and has made an effort to blame Dean for it."

"So different and so similar," Charles said with a chuckle. "And then we have an angry ex-girlfriend who worked for years to pay off the debt he left her in."

Avery had never seen Deb as an actual suspect, and her stomach turned to hear her mentioned in the conversation. She refused to believe Charles actually thought Deb could have done it. "Oh no," Avery said. "Deb is not really a suspect in this, according to me."

"She's your friend," Charles shrugged. "But one thing I've learned is that all of us have the ability to murder."

Avery didn't like that one bit. And she knew how stubborn Charles could be about that kind of thing, but she wouldn't even entertain it in the conversation.

"She can't be the murderer," Avery said. "She's terrible at keeping secrets. She would have told one of us if she had done it. Probably more than one of us! You can't really think she's capable of something like this?" Avery waved in the direction of the guest house, and Charles let out a soft chuckle.

"No, of course, I agree with you," he said. "I don't think she could have done it either. But she is still listed as a suspect, so she is still part of the investigation. Until her name is removed from the official suspect list, she must continue to be treated like one."

Avery hated it when Charles was right. But she thought the fact that Deb was still a suspect was ridiculous. There were two people with even stronger motives. If they were still looking into Deb, they were wasting their time.

"You need to not see her as a friend for a moment," Charles said. "Picture her as just another character in a book. Then look at what Dean did to her and how she suffered because of it. You have to admit that she is a good suspect."

"Absolutely not," Avery said. "Even as a character in my book. Deb is everywhere all the time, and she knows everybody. She has no concept of remaining under the radar with anything. I'm not saying she couldn't be a murderer; I'm just saying that there's no way she would get away with it for this long."

"Do you think she'd break?" Charles asked with an amused smile.

"I heard how she spoke about her time in jail," Avery said.

"She was bored. I think she would have broken just to make it more interesting for herself."

Charles burst out laughing at the thought of it. Avery felt terrible for saying it. But Deb had always had a very low tolerance for things that were boring.

"Why is she still a suspect anyway?" Avery asked. "There are multiple people who can confirm having seen her at the wedding all night."

"We're a small town," Charles said. "And nobody liked him. The police can't be certain that her friends wouldn't cover for her. So, even with the confirmed alibis, anybody with a strong enough motive will remain on the suspect list until there is concrete proof that there is absolutely no way they could have done it."

"Our witness statements aren't enough?" she asked as she took another sip of her wine.

"Nope," Charles shook his head. "That kind of crime didn't necessarily take long. And the venue isn't far from here. The police believe it is entirely possible that she could've snuck out of the wedding for fifteen to twenty minutes without anybody noticing."

"You might be right," Avery said. "We were all too busy watching you hug that bottle of merlot."

Charles did his best not to blush, but Avery knew she had embarrassed him. She didn't intend to keep bringing it up. It had just been so funny, and having seen the video footage earlier that day, she was reminded of it. She couldn't let it go just yet.

"At least I was dancing," Charles teased. "You sat on the sideline. How boring of you."

"That's because I know what I look like when I dance," Avery said. "And it is not pretty. It was to the benefit of everyone present that I remained in my seat at all times."

"If you say so," Charles said with a shrug.

Avery frowned. She understood Charles' explanation about why Deb was still a suspect. But she still didn't agree. She thought it was absurd that the police were willing to use any of their resources on Deb.

"Deb couldn't have left the party without us knowing it," Avery said. "She was all over the place and talking to everyone. We would have noticed if the room had suddenly fallen quiet." Charles let out a snort, but Avery wasn't certain she was joking. It had happened before with Deb at other parties.

"Well, unless we can provide concrete proof that there wasn't a single moment when she left the wedding party, then she will remain a suspect until all of this is solved and the real murderer has been caught."

Their dinner was finished, and Charles helped Avery clean up as he always did. Then she carried Sprinkles inside as she waved Charles goodbye.

It was a pleasant night and quiet, and Avery wasn't even nearly sleepy enough to go to bed yet. So, she browsed her stack of movies to see if anything tickled her fancy. There were a few, so she pulled them all out of the shelf and decided to start at the top and see how far she got before she fell asleep. Sprinkles made himself comfortable at her feet, and she poured herself another glass of wine. But she could hardly concentrate on the movie. She kept thinking about what Charles had said. And she started to look at the suspects as if they were book characters and not actual people.

Carl, the police officer, had a good motive. He might have had the strength to break the door down, too. Although Charles felt it wasn't an important point. Still, he was a police officer at heart. Of all the people on the suspect list, he was the one whose entire career had been about protecting people. But Avery knew that cops had killed before, and it wasn't entirely unheard of. She had too little information on him, though. As a character, he was a little empty. She didn't know his age or his description. All she knew was that the victim had cost him his job and ruined his life.

Then, there was Simon, the bookstore owner. Dean had not yet done him wrong but had intended to, according to Simon. His family-run business had been in that building and part of his family going back for generations. They were a tourist attraction for the town. Simon had a large family and a lot of mouths to feed. As the sole breadwinner, he would have lost a lot if Dean had gone through with the sale.

That left Deb for last. She was an angry ex-girlfriend. Dean had stolen from her and gotten away with it. The result of that had cost Carl his job. It wasn't entirely impossible that more than one person was involved, but it seemed unlikely to her.

There had been no witnesses to the murder itself. But she knew that there had been other guests there that night. Some of them had reported hearing the loud sound of the door breaking, but none of them had heard any kind of chatter.

That seemed unusual for a group crime. No, it had to be one single person.

And she knew that it couldn't be Deb. Deb just didn't seem to be the right character for that kind of murder. Ex-girl-friends don't smother their ex-boyfriends. Not after every-thing he had put her through. Scorned women were brutal. She didn't fit. Avery knew that she had to get Deb's name off the suspect list somehow without interfering too much in the investigation itself. And it all rested on her alibi. It was sound but just not sound enough.

She felt the pressure growing on her shoulders as she thought about her friends. Deb needed her name cleared so she could move on with her life and forget about Dean entirely. And Eleanor needed the murder to be solved so the newlyweds could go on their expensive honeymoon.

The sound of a text on her phone distracted her from her thoughts. It was from Charles.

Thank you for a lovely dinner. If that is my bonus, then I will put in extra work whenever you need it!

Avery chuckled. She stared at the television for a while as her brain numbed itself with thoughts on how to clear Deb's name. It did nothing to ease her stress, but it did an excellent job of lulling her to sleep. Avery and Sprinkles slept deeply on the couch until the sound of the movie title screen startled her awake, and she dragged her feet to her bedroom.

Chapter Twelve

It was way too early in the morning when Avery started to wake up. The summer sun was beaming in through the gap in the curtain earlier than it usually did. It did a good job of waking Sprinkles up. Avery tried to ignore the sunlight and the hyperactive golden retriever, but she hadn't slept very well at all.

She figured that if she just kept her eyes closed and stayed as still as possible, both the sun and Sprinkles would leave her to sleep for another half an hour. It was a plan she had tried many times before, and it had never worked. But Avery knew that she would try it anyway again and again.

Sprinkles had already been awake for some time, so he was whining for her to open the door to the backyard. She knew that once he had become that awake, there was no way to get him back to sleep again. It was a lost cause.

And even if she could, the gap in the curtains had angled the ray of sun to shine perfectly across her eyes. Her bed was comfortable, but the sun in her eyes took every ounce of comfort that she once had away.

Avery gave up. She rolled out of bed and rubbed her eyes

as Sprinkles came to greet her. He hopped up on the bed and snuggled into her neck, and she could feel his wagging tail as it slapped softly against the mattress.

"Okay, okay," she whispered. "I'm up...kinda."

Avery stumbled with blurred vision to the door leading to the backyard and pulled it open. Sprinkles ran out as fast as he could and bounced around. She had fallen asleep earlier than usual the night before, and she wondered why it was that she felt so tired.

It almost felt as if she hadn't had any sleep at all. Her eyes burned, and she could feel how puffy they were every time she blinked.

Oh yes. The dreams. She had dreamed terrible dreams for the majority of the night. Most of them involved the doors to her home being broken down by someone that she couldn't quite see. And then, after that, she had dreams of Deb being dragged away in handcuffs for a crime she hadn't committed. Somewhere in the mix of it, she dreamed of Eleanor and Samuel cooking themselves a very depressed Spanish meal in their home to cheer themselves up after having to completely cancel their honeymoon.

She watched as Sprinkles rolled in the grass without a care in the world. The sky was the perfect blue, and not a single cloud was present. She knew it was going to be a hot day. So, she decided that to clear her head, she would head out for a walk in the vineyard before the sun became too intense for her.

She rushed back in to fix herself a cup of coffee and get dressed for a walk. Then, she called Sprinkles and motioned for him to follow her. The vines were lush and stood proudly in the morning sun. She brushed her hands through the bright green leaves around her. It was time to have them pruned. The vines looked better that year than they had ever looked, and she was expecting a very successful wine season. It made her proud to think of it. But then there was the mark on her pride.

A murder had taken place on her farm just a few days ago. She looked at the ground the vines grew in and thought of the hole at the cemetery where Dean's body would be laid to rest. For the vines, the earth meant life. But for Dean, the earth meant death.

She called for Sprinkles to stay close to her, and he followed her instruction without hesitation. Then, she practiced some of his new tricks with him. He had learned some of them only the day before, and still, he was performing them almost perfectly.

He always had a smile when she was giving him orders. Even when they were out in public, it was as if he enjoyed it. It made her think of his behavior at the bookstore again, and it just didn't sit right with her. He hadn't begged for food the night before when he lay right at the table. She'd eaten a fair share of sandwiches around Sprinkles, and not once had he shown any interest in it at all. She found it hard to believe that Simon's sandwich was so good that it completely made Sprinkles lose his manners. Then again, she didn't have any other explanation for it.

She continued with their practicing as they carried on with their walk through the vineyard. She thought about how many years she'd spent away from the vineyard when she and James lived in the city. As a young woman, she had rejected the idea of running it entirely. But she was grateful her parents insisted that she come back. It was the first time in her life that she felt truly proud of what she was doing.

The breeze was cool and fresh as it washed over them and felt like a comforting embrace across her warm skin. The breeze disturbed some butterflies that had been hidden among the vines, and they fluttered through the sky like confetti.

She looked back toward her home and the guest house, and for the first time, she didn't only think of the crime scene. All of it felt a lot better since Charles had made the room right for her again. She decided that she would reopen the farm for customers the next day. She couldn't leave it any longer. She'd had enough success that the few days they'd been closed hadn't hurt her too badly financially. But she couldn't remain closed for too long. Everything needed to continue as it once had.

Everyone had worked tirelessly to create a successful season, and she didn't want to let them all down. She looked across the vineyard and knew that it deserved to be celebrated.

She reached into her back pocket and pulled out her phone. The screen was tough to see in the bright light, but she navigated her way around quite easily. She opened the chat that included all the staff of the farm and let them know to return to work in the morning. She was certain that not all of them would be as excited about it as she was, but that was the tough part of being somebody's boss.

Before she slipped her phone back into her pocket, a stream of messages came through. They flooded her screen, and they were all coming from the same person. Eleanor had sent her almost forty photographs followed by one sentence.

I've received the first photographs of the wedding!

The photographs just kept coming through, and for a moment, Avery considered just switching her phone off. The buzzing just wouldn't stop, and already some of the other Stammtisch women were commenting on it all. She didn't even know where to begin. But Sprinkles was occupied by a loose branch that had fallen to the ground, and she thought she would let him play for a while.

She started at the top and worked her way down. Most of them were the average wedding photographs. Beautifully dressed people all standing in a line right next to each other, putting on their best smiles. Then there were some photographs from the ceremony. They looked like any other wedding, too. Every wedding that Avery had ever been to had resulted in the same sequence of photographs. Still, she loved to see Samuel and Eleanor so happy.

Avery paused when a photograph of Sprinkles walking proudly down the aisle with the ring pillow in his mouth came past. He had a large smile on his face, and every face that was visible in the background behind him wore an equally big smile.

She immediately made the photograph of Sprinkles her phone wallpaper and sent it on to Charles before looking at the next one. There were photographs of people dancing, making speeches, and enjoying a good meal.

It made her happy to see that every person photographed had a glass of her wine in their hands too. There were too many photographs for her to pay attention to all of them, and she wondered how much more there would be if Eleanor said that these were only the first.

Avery was grateful that the photographer hadn't snapped any photographs of the police intruding on the party. She imagined how Eleanor and Samuel might have reacted to being so frequently reminded of the event.

Then it made her laugh a little as she pictured an album filled with beautifully-dressed people being confronted by the police and all their shocked faces. If it wasn't someone she cared about whom it had happened to, she might have wanted to see something like that.

The sun was beating down on her, and she could feel her skin starting to burn. She looked around for a spot of shade but felt nothing. The earth beneath her feet was also getting warm already, and she had a lot to do if she wanted to reopen the next day.

Sprinkles looked like he was having fun, and she hated to put an end to it. But they couldn't stay out there forever. She could last a few more minutes, though. She watched Sprinkles roll around in the dirt before he got distracted by a passing butterfly. He sat upright and watched as it fluttered daintily past his eyes. Then, the butterfly came to a stop on the tip of his nose. Avery had never seen him stand so still. She opened the camera app on her phone and did her best to approach him as carefully as she could.

She got Sprinkles and the butterfly in the frame and focused, but just as she was about to snap the photograph, the butterfly took off again. Sprinkles sneezed as if he had been holding it in so as not to disturb the butterfly.

Avery raced to check the photographs on her phone to see if she had successfully captured the moment, and as she did so, she realized how she could clear Deb's name and remove her from the suspect list completely.

She urgently motioned for Sprinkles to join her as she walked as fast as possible back toward her home. As she walked, Avery considered all the ways in which her plan could work or not work. It would take her some time, and she needed to make sure that it was guaranteed to work.

As soon as she was through the door and back in the cool shade of her own home, she texted the women of the Stammtisch and summoned them to help her with her plan.

Chapter Thirteen

Avery had her laptop on the passenger seat as she drove over to Charles' house. She felt bad calling him so out of the blue. It wasn't her favorite thing to just drop in on people like that. But the women of the Stammtisch had worked hard all day on a way to clear Deb's name.

The directions to Charles' house were scribbled on a small piece of paper which she held in her fingers as she navigated the streets to his house. She felt a little excited at the thought that perhaps by the time she left his house, Deb's name would be cleared.

She hoped it worked, she didn't have any other idea, and she knew Deb was innocent. Avery didn't want the police to spend too much time looking into her as a suspect while the real killer was still somewhere out there.

As usual, because she was in a hurry, it seemed to take her forever to get anywhere. Every car ahead of her was slow, and it seemed like everything was trying to stop her from actually getting to his house. But she took a deep breath. Another twenty minutes won't end the world.

But although her mind was behaving logically, her hands

still felt clammy, and her heart still began to race as she did her best to find her patience.

When she eventually pulled into Charles' driveway, it occurred to her for the first time, that she had never seen the inside of his house. She wondered what it would look like inside and tried her best to picture it.

But when he opened the door, it was nothing like she had imagined it would be. His home was filled with antique furniture and smelled of wood polish. One large sofa filled most of the living room, and every surface was piled up with either books or newspapers.

On one wall, there was a bookshelf that covered the entirety of it, and the bookshelf was crammed full of movies. He lived alone, and she knew his family never lived nearby. It had never crossed her mind what he might be doing to pass all that time alone in his home.

His house was clean, but there was stuff all over the place. There seemed to be no true décor style or system of any kind for organization. There was a freedom about it that Avery was almost envious of. But what she was most envious of were the large windows in his kitchen.

His stove had a view of the vineyards that nearly took her breath away. She imagined the meals she might create if she could look out over a view like that every time she cooked.

I should put some more windows in my kitchen.

"You said you have something important to show me that would clear Deb's name?" he said cheerfully, handing her a can of soda.

"Yes," she said with a smile. "Where is the best place for us to sit?"

She tapped the laptop bag that hung over her shoulder to imply that she needed a table, and he ushered her into his dining room, where a large eight-seater table sat covered in more books and stacks of photographs.

At the far end of the dining room was a large wine rack filled with bottles. And she recognized some of the labels. He had an extensive collection—one that she was certain was worth a fair amount of money. It seemed funny to her that, even though she had known him so long, she had learned more about him in the short walk through his home than she had learned in years of conversation with him.

Charles cleared a space on the table for her, and she set up her laptop. Then she opened the folder that they'd put together and paged him through an organized sequence of photographs and video clips. Each of them had a time stamp, and through that, there were only about three minutes of the night where Deb was unaccounted for in the photographs.

It proved that she had never left the wedding. And as Avery showed it to him, she felt quite proud.

Nestled between the stacks of books and newspapers, she noticed that it was a perfect scene for a crime novel detective to find herself in. She made a mental note of what the space looked like. She wanted to add it to her notes later. Charles' home would be the perfect home for her main character.

"This is great," he said, looking quite pleased. "This should do the trick. We should get this down to the station immediately."

"Excellent," Avery said with a small cheer. "We can take my car; I'll drive."

The police looked through it all and then copied every item from her laptop over onto their own drive to take in as evidence.

"This can't have been quick or easy to put together," the officer said to her.

"Of course not," she answered. "But it had to be done.

The longer you look into her, the longer it takes to find the real culprit."

"You are correct there," the police officer laughed. "Well, I'll give Deb a call then and let her know that we will no longer be treating her as a suspect, but I'm sure she expects the call."

"Probably," Avery laughed. "She helped us put it all together!"

Avery felt a huge amount of pride as she watched them make the phone call, and Avery noticed a large smile on Charles' face as well. She refused to leave until they had confirmed completely and to her liking that Deb would no longer be questioned as a suspect in the murder. Only when she was entirely satisfied did Charles convince her that it was time to go and leave the officers alone to do their jobs. By the time she and Charles walked out, the sun was already setting, and it would soon be night.

"That leaves only three suspects left, for now," Charles said.

"I don't know if I can handle it if this gets any more complicated," Avery laughed. "I'd like to stick to three suspects, please."

"Unfortunately, that's not how this works," he chuckled. "But for now, we only have three."

"So, that leaves Mrs. Scott, the victim's mother, Simon from the bookstore, and the ex-cop that my father was talking about," Avery said.

"Yes, that's it for now," Charles said. "I had a look into that friend of your father's. Carl Brown is his name. I couldn't find much about him, only what your father told us about. Any information after he left the force seems vague."

"Did you ask some of the other officers?" she asked. "Maybe they knew him?"

"I did," he answered. "Nobody really knew him very well; they mostly just knew *of* him, that's all. But we'll find out more somehow. We have to. He's a suspect."

When they arrived back at Charles' house, he invited her to dinner at his place for the first time. And when they walked in, she saw how the setting sun had created a bright, golden glow throughout his kitchen.

She wondered if she could ever just cook one meal there as she watched over the setting sun.

"It'll have to be pizza," he said. "I'm afraid I don't cook much at all."

"You don't cook?!" she asked, shocked. "In here?!" Avery waved through the space with her arms. It was a large kitchen that had clearly been designed by someone who loved to cook. "You're breaking my heart," she teased. "But pizza will be just fine."

Charles ordered the pizza, and when he came back, he had a bottle of wine in his hand. He reached into a cabinet and retrieved two beautiful antique crystal glasses. In between the heaps of papers and old books, Avery enjoyed one of the most luxurious glasses of wine she'd ever had. It was well-balanced, not too heavy on the tannins, and had a slight lingering jamminess on the finish.

"How is it going with the book planning?" he asked her.

Avery sighed. "James used to make it look so easy," she said. "I have all these notes I've made of things I want to include and ideas that I have, and I just have no idea how I'm supposed to stitch them all together."

"I'm sure it will stitch itself together," he said.

"Well, what's worse, is that I have all these pieces of papers with one-liners scribbled down on them," she explained as she took another sip. "I keep waking up at night with what I think are these perfectly sculpted words and descriptions, then I rush to write them down, and when I look at them again, I think they're absolute garbage."

"Even garbage has its place in this world," Charles teased. "Every item in my home was once cast out by another home, I guess."

"I suppose," Avery said. "I mean, I'm not sure anybody ever saw any of it as garbage, but I suppose if someone wanted to keep it, they would have."

"I saw you looking at the collection of your husband's books at the bookstore the other day," he said softly. "He's quite popular in our little town, you know. I have a fair collection of his books myself. In fact, there's a character in one of them that reminds me a lot of you." He pointed to a small bookshelf, and she saw that the entire bottom row was packed with her husband's publications.

"I know you were a part of his process," Charles said plainly. "So, I'm certain you'll be brilliant at it."

Avery wasn't certain what to say, so she sat in brief silence until the doorbell rang to announce that their dinner had arrived. As she waited for Charles to come back with their pizza, she realized that she felt comfortable in his home. Something about being surrounded by books and movies reminded her of how quiet her life had become. There was a time when that scared her, but she had grown to love that silence. And Charles' home was very quiet.

She knew that if he ever did feel the need to occupy his mind with something, he would only need to reach out his arm and grab the nearest thing to him, and it would be filled with words and images to get his mind turning.

"I hope you're hungry," he said. "Because I never eat the leftovers. I always forget I have them."

He placed the pizzas down on the table and filled her glass again, and it seemed just so much like Charles to drink expensive wine while chewing on delivery pizza. And that was the small nuance about him that she liked most.

He was the perfect blend of sophistication and practicality. It made him an excellent friend, and if she were entirely honest, the wine and food paired excellently.

The two of them sat together and spoke about their favorite books and films long after the food had been finished. His home seemed like a treasure chest to her, and she knew that if she opened a cupboard or spent enough time looking at any one shelf or surface, she would find yet another item of interest to her.

When she finally left to go home, she felt as if she had entirely left the world for the few hours that she had been there. She hoped he'd invite her back again and that the next time, she'd feel more comfortable searching through his collection of items. She knew she would find inspiration for her book there, and already she could imagine the scenes that she wanted, and when she finally stepped into her own home again, she found the spaces rather boring.

Chapter Fourteen

Avery had spent most of the previous evening unpacking old boxes full of books and arranging them on her bookshelf. There were books in there she'd forgotten she'd ever read at all, and it made her feel both happy and sad.

Next to her bed lay a pile of books she'd put there with the intention of reading them again. She liked the way it made her home look when it was full of books. It reminded her of the home she'd had with her husband. Not too long ago, she'd been convinced that she would never be able to face it all again. She had been so convinced that it would make her feel sad and cause her to grieve again. But it was better than the room full of closed boxes that she had been living with before. She understood now that there was no point in pretending her life before had never existed.

With her favorite belongings once again decorating the space around her, she had slept through the night without disruption until Sprinkles had woken her up again. And the more the year progressed, the more often that was happening.

But that morning, when she had woken up in her home, filled with the belongings of her old life, she missed her husband. But it wasn't in a bad way. It was a positive desire, she felt, to be reminded of him and all that they had together before. So, she hopped in her car and headed back to the bookstore. She wanted to see if any of her husband's books had more notes in them from those who had owned them before.

She hadn't really considered how his books might have impacted the lives of the people who read them. She'd only ever known how they had impacted hers. And when she walked into the bookstore that day, it didn't remind her of her childhood anymore. Instead, it reminded her of Charles and his home.

She looked around and wondered how many of the books in that store would wind up in his home one day and how many of them she'd be buying for him. She walked to the shelf with her husband's books on it and started taking them off the shelf. Some of them had notes to loved ones on the first page, and others simply just had a name and a year. Avery realized as she paged through them that some books, must have belonged to crime novel lovers, as they had penciled in questions and notes all along the sides of the page.

She remembered an argument between her mother and father that she'd overheard once as a child. Her mother felt it was a sin to write in a book and that the pages should have been kept pristine. However, her father argued that the author of the book wanted the reader to enjoy it in any which way they pleased. He had said that the moment he opened the book, it was ruined. And so, he was free to write in it if he liked. And Avery quite liked the way the pencil notes looked alongside her husband's writing. She hoped that someone would write in her book someday.

"Good morning, Avery," Simon greeted her. "No dog with you today?"

"Unfortunately not," Avery said, somewhat wary of Simon as a suspect. "He's at the groomers today."

"That's a pity!" Simon answered. "I have an especially delicious sandwich here today."

Avery let out an uneasy chuckle as Simon held up the sandwich he had stashed away behind the counter. She thought about asking him what was on it. She wanted to know what was so delicious that it had caused her well-trained Sprinkles to lose all his manners.

But she wasn't too interested in starting a conversation with him. She couldn't be certain that she wouldn't ask him a question related to the case. Avery couldn't risk that, it would only be interfering, and she liked Simon and his shop. If she started asking questions, she ran the risk of discovering that it was true and that he was not the person she thought he was at all.

But when he held out the sandwich, she noticed an unmissable fragility in his hand. His hand appeared swollen and weak, unlike anything she'd seen before. Her eyes had lingered too long on his impediment, and he had noticed the question burning silently in her mind.

"I have arthritis," he said with a kind smile. "I was diagnosed about a year ago, and I'm afraid it's progressing faster than even I'd like to believe."

"I'm really sorry to hear that, Simon," Avery said.

"It's alright, mostly," he said. "And I like to think the treatments will get better sooner than we think...thankfully, this job doesn't require all that much strength."

"I suppose that's lucky," she said with a nervous laugh. "I've always thought it must be quite pleasant to work in the bookstore."

"It is," Simon said with a wide smile. "And although my health deteriorates, my lovely wife stays as healthy and strong as ever. She has become my hands now, you see. I barely have enough grip left to screw in a lightbulb."

It was such a common, everyday task that the rest of the world took it completely for granted. And at that moment, Avery wondered who would care for her when she could no longer do it. It seemed a paranoid thought, but she'd always assumed she'd be capable and alright on her own.

Nobody expects their strength to fail them. Her parents had each other, and Simon had his wife to screw in the lightbulb for him. If she got arthritis one day, would she be forever doomed to live in the dark?

Another customer, thankfully, took Simon's attention away from her. To avoid getting roped into another conversation with him or completely plunging into the depths about the small possibility that she might not be able to change her own lightbulb someday, she walked up the spiral staircase and disappeared onto the upper floor.

Her eyes caught the row of cookbooks, and immediately, she thought back to Charles' perfect kitchen. It bothered her tremendously that he never used it to cook. In fact, she could see that the stove and oven had barely been touched in years. With that in mind, she set off on a mission to find him the perfect cookbook. At the very least, it would make him laugh. And at best, he could cook a meal for her.

She browsed through all the countries and types of food, and none of them really stood out to her as something Charles might show any kind of interest in. That's when she spotted a cookbook with a spine that was taped together.

There was no longer a name or author on the spine at all, and the pages seemed stained by food and wine. She pulled it from the shelf, and it fell open on a specific page. It must have been the original owner's favorite recipe.

It didn't take her long to realize it was a pizza recipe book.

And it was perfect for him. She looked over the pages, growing hungrier by the second as she gazed over all the delicious recipes.

She tucked the book under her arm and made the decision that it would be the perfect gift for Charles. But she'd have to go downstairs and speak to Simon again. Avery thought about his shaking hand and how he had no strength left and made a note to research how one got the disease as soon as she got home. If there was some way that she could avoid it, she intended to do just that. But when she heard the sound of the door creaking from another customer entering the store, it dawned on her. If he wasn't strong enough to screw in a lightbulb, then there was no way that he could have broken down the door to Dean's room. Neither would he have had the strength to smother Dean.

She breathed a sigh of relief, knowing that it dramatically cut down their suspect list to only two people, which meant they could solve the crime, and her two newlywed friends could make it on time for their honeymoon.

She happily made her way back down the spiral staircase to pay for the book. She said goodbye to Simon, wishing him the best of luck with the disease, and within a few minutes, she was pulling into the driveway at her own home.

But a nagging voice in her mind said she needed more proof that Simon couldn't have done it. She looked at the entrance to the guest house. It was an old cellar that they no longer used, and it had become a rather popular guest house. But there were still some empty rooms, and she decided that she would test the door to see how easy it was to break it down. She risked doing damage to the property, but if they were easy enough for her to break, then she had bigger problems on her hands. Avery wanted to know her guests were safe. She never wanted to learn that a murder had occurred on her property ever again. So, she went in and checked which room was empty. She picked one all the way at the end to avoid bothering any of the existing customers that were there.

Staring at the door, Avery realized she had no idea where to begin if she wanted to break a door down. She remembered the movies she'd seen, so she moved back and tried to ram it down with her shoulder. But that only resulted in a sharp-shooting pain, and the door barely budged. She kicked it, tried running up to it, and still, the door didn't budge. She was pleased that her guest house was safer than she thought, but she was also certain she had bruised herself in a few places. Out of breath and out of ideas, she concluded that Simon could certainly not have broken down the door and decided to let Charles know of the new information she had received.

Simon couldn't have done it. He has arthritis and no strength left. That leaves only Mrs. Scott and Carl. Let me know when I can call to tell you what I know.

P.S. I have a new book for your collection.

She read through the message twice until she was satisfied that it was good enough and then sent it along. And it wasn't long before he responded with a time for her to call him. She paged through the pizza recipe book she had bought him and wrote down some of the ones that she also wanted to keep.

When she decided it was time for a glass of wine, she felt oddly disappointed to see a shocking lack of antique crystal in her cabinets. *That'll have to change.* But she settled for her average wine glass and poured herself a chilled glass of chenin blanc before making herself as comfortable as possible on the sofa.

She spent the rest of her evening paging through the

recipe book while her favorite movie played on the television, only getting up to refill her wine from time to time. Sprinkles sniffed the books on her shelf eagerly, his tail wagging as he enjoyed the new décor.

It was a perfectly pleasant evening as the warm summer air wafted in through the windows, creating the perfect atmosphere after a hot summer's day.

When she finally rested her head on her pillow, she stared at the lightbulb that was nested neatly in her ceiling lamp and sighed. *Who will change you when I no longer can?*

Chapter Fifteen

Avery looked through the notes she'd made for her book and saw that two suspects had been crossed off the list. The ex-girlfriend and the bookstore owner had red lines through them. Something about it was incredibly satisfying to her, and already her story didn't seem so all over the place anymore.

There were two more names on the suspect list, and she was eager to find out which one of them would do it. It felt strange to look at a case that was currently unfurling and see it as a story that she was piecing together; it gave her an odd perspective on the entire thing.

She flipped through the stack of pages, going over all the ideas she had already accumulated, wondering if, somewhere in there, the answer was already obvious. All they needed to do was narrow it down to one of the two people left on the page and hope that another suspect didn't make themselves known.

How hard could it be?

She scoffed at that thought when she remembered all the manuscripts James had thrown into the trash because there were too many questions with impossible answers or too many issues with continuity. He had always told her that even the perfect story had the potential to fall apart completely. The difference, though, was that her story was happening on her own doorstep, and she could watch it and learn. The questions would eventually answer themselves, and anything that happened would be completely possible because hers was based on something true.

Her phone buzzed, and instinctively, she reached to check who the text was from.

The police just phoned. We're free to go on our honeymoon, provided we answer if they call. We'll see you all in two weeks!

Attached was a photograph from Eleanor of their two suitcases, packed and waiting at the door. The Stammtisch group chat exploded with excited responses, and Avery was pleased they could make it after all. They deserved a happy honeymoon after everything they had been through.

A cold, wet nose was pressed against her ankle as Sprinkles came to ask her to open the door for him. She checked her watch, and saw there was still some time before she was expected to call Charles and tell him what she'd learned about Simon.

So, she took her time to sip a cup of coffee out in the backyard as Sprinkles played with anything he could find lying on the lawn. The sun had already warmed the ground, and the birds were chirping merrily in the trees above her.

She looked out over the sunny lawn and wished she could make herself comfortable there all day with a good book and some good food. It would be the perfect day—just her and Sprinkles, the sun, and the birds. The only thing that would have made it better was if a cool breeze arrived to cool them down.

The sound of her phone ringing canceled out her daydream, and she rushed inside to see that she'd been late to phone Charles, and he was phoning her instead.

"Charles, sorry," she answered. "I was outside with Sprinkles."

"It's a beautiful day outside," he said cheerfully.

She walked with her phone and sat down on one of her patio chairs, watching as Sprinkles attempted to herd the birds back into their tree.

"So, tell me about Simon," Charles said.

She told him about the tremor in his hand and his weakness. And Charles agreed that someone that weak couldn't possibly have broken the door down or suffocated the victim, as both things required some strength.

"And that should be easy enough to verify; we just need to speak to his wife and get some proof...a pharmacy receipt for his medication or something," he said.

She scribbled it down to add to her ever-growing pile of notes. "That's a good idea. And that leaves us with only two more suspects on the list."

"You are correct," Charles said. "We've got the victim's mother and your father's friend, Carl."

"I think they should bring Carl in for questioning next," she said.

"They are reluctant to do so for two reasons," he explained. "Carl is the only one on the suspect list that actually wasn't a guest at the wedding, and they have no evidence to arrest him. Apparently, when they phoned to speak to him the other day, he refused to answer any of their questions."

"That seems a little unfriendly," Avery said.

"Well, he knows his rights, and I don't think he's been

fond of the police ever since he was forced out of his job," Charles answered.

"And what about Mrs. Scott?" Avery asked.

"She's a grieving mother," Charles said. "So, they're approaching her carefully. She has enough money to sue the department into bankruptcy if she were so inclined."

"I might have an idea to get some information regarding Carl's involvement in this; let me see what I can do," Avery said as she swallowed the last sip of her coffee.

"Just don't do anything that could get us into trouble," Charles said. "He's smarter than you think about all of this, and I don't want to scare him away."

"Of course," Avery said. "I wouldn't do such a thing. I'll leave the heavy work to the police. We just need enough information to warrant an arrest, right?"

"That's right," Charles said. "And it has to be obtained legally. So, we either need a statement from him or a witness who is willing to testify."

She understood perfectly. So when she ended the call, she got dressed as quickly as she could and made the pleasant walk to the end of the property to visit her parents. But it wasn't so easy to stick to the topic at hand.

"What's with all those empty boxes in the trash?" her mother asked as she handed Avery a cup of coffee.

"I unpacked some of my old books," Avery answered. "Why are you taking note of what's in the trash?"

"Your mother can't help herself," her father said, entering the kitchen without greeting. "She doesn't miss a thing, I tell you. I've never gotten away with anything in my life."

"It just seems odd, is all," her mother continued. "You've had those boxes in storage for so long. Why unpack them now?"

Avery stared blankly at her mother as she took a sip of

coffee. "That's not important. I've actually come here to ask Dad a favor."

Despite it having little to do with her mother, the elderly lady sat down at the table and paid full attention. Her father didn't seem to mind or care—he'd gotten used to it after so many years of marriage.

"I'll do anything for you, dear, you know that," he said with a kind smile. "Do I need to get my toolbox?"

"No, it's not that kind of favor," Avery asked.

Without hesitation, her father reached for his wallet, and Avery put out her hand to stop him. "And it's nothing like that either, Dad. I haven't needed money from you for almost twenty years now."

"Well, if it's not handy work, and it's not money, what is it then?" he said, looking completely lost.

"Your friend, Carl, that you told us about the other day at the bookstore. Do you remember?" she asked.

"Yes, of course," he answered with a shrug.

"Well, because of what you told us about how his life was ruined by Dean Scott and how he always blamed Dean for everything that had gone wrong with him...he's made it to the suspect list in the murder case," Avery explained.

"They're accusing him of murder?!" he said, raising his voice.

Her father frowned so deeply that the wrinkles of his face almost completely covered his eyes, and all Avery could see were the folds of skin and gray eyebrows.

"They're not accusing him of murder yet," Avery said calmly. "But they do suspect him of it, given the way he feels about the victim."

"That is an outrage," her father said, slamming his hand on the counter.

"Oh, calm down, love," her mother interrupted him. "It

can't come as such a surprise to you. I think he's a good suspect."

"You barely know the man," her father argued.

"Perhaps that's better," her mother said. "Who wants to be friends with a murderer?"

"He's not a murderer," her father insisted. "And I don't understand what it is you expect me to do about any of this."

"Well, he's not being easy with the police," Avery explained. "I was hoping that you could go and visit him and just find out one small bit of information somehow."

"And what might that be?" her father asked as he crossed his arms. "Do you want me to walk into my friend's house and ask him if he murdered someone on my property?"

"No," Avery said. "And I certainly don't want you to be so direct about any of this either. I simply want you to find out where he was on the night of the wedding. And work it into the conversation...don't be so obvious."

"Oh, please," her mother laughed. "Your father is the most obvious man on Earth. He knows nothing about being discreet. I knew about the engagement ring weeks before he proposed. I kept seeing the box in his pocket!"

"That doesn't matter anyway," her father argued. "Because I won't do it. He is my friend, and I won't insult him like that."

"Don't think of it as trying to prove his guilt, Dad," Avery said. "Think of it as trying to prove his innocence. If we can prove his whereabouts were nowhere near the guest house on the night of the murder, then you have saved him from a great deal of trouble."

There was a pause in the conversation as her father thought it through. He was a stubborn man, and she knew he might need a little more convincing than that, but that was her best argument.

"He'll do it," her mother said.

"You can't decide that for me," her father snapped.

"Yes, I can, and I have," her mother said. "You are going to visit him; you've been meaning to do so for some time, and you are going to help him clear his name of this. It's what a good friend would do."

In the end, Avery didn't have to argue any further. As it had been her entire life, her mother was the deciding voice, and her father agreed to set up a visit with Carl.

"Right, then, that's settled," her mother said. "So tell me about the books. Why have you unpacked them now?"

Avery's jaw dropped. After everything they had just discussed, her mother was still more interested in her personal life.

"I just missed them, that's all," Avery eventually answered. She didn't want to give more detail than that, so she swallowed what was left of her coffee and said her farewells before heading to the wine room to let Charles know of her plan.

It was a busy day at the vineyard that day, and Avery hardly had any more time to look at her book or piece together what little amount of her story she already had. And by the time the sun started to set, she and Sprinkles walked slowly together through the vines, enjoying the silence as she sipped on some velvety merlot.

The bright orange of the sun cast rays up from behind the green vines, creating what was easily one of the most spectacular sunsets that Avery had seen in a long time. She wondered if the sunsets in Spain would be just as beautiful and how much longer Eleanor and Samuel had to wait before they reached their destination.

Even Sprinkles had stopped to admire the sunset, his ears perked and tail wagging as Avery went to stand beside him.

Chapter Sixteen

Although it was completely dark outside, the air was still warm. Avery washed the dishes after cooking dinner and dreamed about one day having a view to look at while she did so. She thought about Charles' kitchen again and wondered how much it would cost to demolish hers and build one exactly like his.

With each passing day, her home was filling up a little more. She'd promised herself that she wouldn't let it get too cluttered. It was Deb that had first suggested she tried minimalism. She'd said it would clear her mind. But the more she unpacked her favorite belongings and put them out on display, the quieter her home seemed to her and the cozier. Suddenly, the color of her sofa didn't bother her so much anymore, and she'd lost the urge to paint and repaint every available wall.

Feeling more at home than ever, Avery made herself comfortable at the dining room table, next to her a list of admin that she needed to catch up with for the vineyard. She was only a little bit behind, but it was a tedious job, and she'd never liked doing it.

Avery had only just gotten started when a knock at the door startled her. With her reading glasses still resting on her nose, she answered and was surprised to see her mother standing alone in the dark with a worried look on her face.

"Where's Dad?" Avery asked, peering behind her mother.

"He's at Carl's house, of course," her mother said, annoyed.

Her mother pushed past her, and she noticed what appeared to be an empty shopping bag hanging over her shoulder. She followed her mother into the living room, where she was already looking through all the freshly unpacked books, checking them for dust.

"Where's your flashlight? You didn't walk in the dark, did you?" Avery asked.

"Pfft," her mother scoffed. "I've been walking that path for so many years now. I could do it blindly."

"You have osteoporosis, Mom," Avery said as she rubbed her eyes. "How many times do we have to go through this? You can't walk in the dark without your flashlight. If you trip over a root, you'll break your hip."

Her mother turned to face her and tapped her hip impatiently. "My hip's fine," she said. "I see you haven't painted this wall yet."

"No, I've decided I will leave it that color," Avery said. "Is there a reason you've dropped by, Mom?"

"Can I not visit my daughter?" her mother asked.

It was clear that something was bothering her mother, and she knew that her mother would come out with it soon enough. But she hadn't bargained on an argument that night and wasn't sure where she'd find the energy to fight it.

Avery sighed. "Alright, well, can I make you some tea or something?"

"Chamomile," her mother answered shortly.

Avery turned to put the kettle on, and as she walked through the entryway into her kitchen, her mother decided that it was the perfect moment to talk about why she had really walked all the way over there in the dark.

"You shouldn't have asked your father to go see Carl," her mother said.

"Mom, *you* encouraged him to do it," Avery said, exasperated. "What made you change your mind? I thought you agreed with me."

She watched as her mother walked along the shelf of books, picking out the ones she found interesting and placing them in the empty bag on her shoulder. And Avery wondered if she'd ever see those books again.

"Well, I did think it was a good idea at the time," her mother said with a shrug. "But that was before I knew how stressed out it would make your father. He's been pacing up and down all day, worrying about what he might say to start the conversation."

"You have got to be kidding," Avery said.

"It's no joke," her mother responded. "You should have seen him. He barely even watched the television today. I've never seen him like that before. It's not fair on him. You know he has a weak heart."

"And you have a weak hip," Avery mumbled.

"I heard that," her mother snapped as she added another book to her collection. "Now, how far are you with that tea?"

Avery made two cups of tea, one for her mother and one for herself. She hoped the tea would calm her down. She didn't want to argue with her mother, but she was being particularly stubborn, and she knew it would be hard.

Thankfully for Avery, the kettle took a while to boil, so she had plenty of time to breathe and compose herself. And by the time she made it back into the living room with the tea, her mother was paging through the notes she had made for her book.

The cups clinked as she placed them on the table, taking the papers from her mother's hand and placing them aside.

"If that was so stressful, he could have just told me," Avery said. "I would have been fine with it if he changed his mind. I was only asking him a favor. He had every right to say no."

"You know your father is too stubborn to do that," her mother answered. "Once he's committed to something, he has to do it. Otherwise, he doesn't sleep at night, and he tosses and turns. It drives me mad!"

You're driving me mad.

Avery felt terrible knowing she had caused her father so much stress. She wished he had told her; she would have stopped him. It was a terrible thing to imagine him pacing through the house, feeling as if he was being forced into something he didn't want to do.

"I'm sorry, Mom," Avery said softly.

Avery's mother looked through the room, her eyes resting on all the items that Avery had recently put out on display. They were items that Avery had brought with her from the city, and although her mother had visited her often there, she looked at them as if she'd never seen them before.

She lifted the photography book that was placed on the center of the table and paged through the first two pages before also adding it to her bag of books. But she noticed that there was something else bothering her mother, and it wasn't anger. Her mother looked really concerned. There was a crease in her brow that Avery had only ever seen when something truly frightened her.

"Is something else bothering you, Mom?" Avery asked,

reaching out to place a hand on her mother's nervously twitching leg.

"I told you that you stressed your father out," her mother said, avoiding eye contact.

"I can see something's wrong, Mom," Avery said softly. "Please, will you tell me about it? You think Dad is the stubborn one?"

Her mother's lips pursed as if she was physically struggling to keep the words in her mouth. She sipped on her tea and pretended to be interested in a decorative ashtray on the side table.

"Mom," Avery said, losing her patience. "What's wrong?"

At last, her mother relaxed her shoulders and put her teacup back on the coffee table.

"I'm worried," her mother said. "Your father left hours ago to see Carl, and he hasn't been answering his phone. He should have been back by now. He completely missed dinner."

"How many times have you phoned him?" Avery asked.

"About five," her mother said. "I keep phoning, and it goes straight to his voicemail message. His phone is off, I think."

Avery didn't like the sound of that one bit. Not only did her father never stay out later than dinner, but on the rare occasion that he did, he was pretty strict about answering his phone. And it wasn't often that he left the house without her mother.

"He told me he was just going for some coffee," her mother said. "I thought he'd be back hours ago already. And he usually lets me know if he's going to be later than expected."

"That is odd," Avery said quietly.

"What if he said something wrong?" her mother broke,

tears threatening to spill. "That man could be a murderer for all we know! What if your father said something wrong and met the same fate as that idiot Dean?"

"I don't understand," Avery said as she rubbed her fingers against her temples in an attempt to stop the inevitable headache. "You were both so certain he was innocent, and now you think it could be him?"

"Your father thought he was innocent," her mother corrected her. "I think he is a very suitable suspect."

"Then why did you say Dad should do it?" Avery said. "Why did you take my side earlier?"

"Because your father said he was innocent, and your father knows him better than me," her mother said. "But the more I think about it, the more I remember that your father has made some terrible judgment calls about people before. Do you remember that man he hired to paint our ceiling? He made off with my pearl earrings!"

"Do you think Dad is in danger?" Avery asked.

"I think it isn't impossible," her mother answered unhelpfully. "It just isn't like him not to answer his phone." Her mother looked like she would burst into tears at any second. Her hands fiddled nervously with the cushion she had pulled onto her lap.

"Why didn't you phone me earlier?" Avery asked.

"I didn't want you to worry," her mother answered.

Avery closed her eyes and turned her head to the heavens, asking for the strength and patience she needed not to lose her temper with her own mother. Then she got up and went to get her phone from where it was placed to charge.

"Alright, well, I'm going to phone him now," she said.

Avery dialed his number, and it didn't even ring. Immediately she heard her father's voice asking for the caller to leave a message after the beep. Her chest tightened as her stomach sank.

"His phone is off," she said.

"I know," her mother answered dryly. "I told you so."

Avery was trying hard not to panic, but it wasn't easy. She could feel a lump in her throat, and already she imagined how her heart would break if her mother's suspicions had been true. She could never live with herself if she had asked her father to visit the man who turned out to be the murderer, and it had gotten him killed.

"Do you know where he went?" Avery asked. "I mean, I know Dad said he's on a nearby farm, but do you have an address for Carl? Did Dad tell you which farm?" Avery was struggling to find the right words to formulate her questions as her stress levels peaked, and her concern for her father's safety caused her brain to scramble.

Her mother reached her shaking hand into her pocket and pulled out a small piece of paper with a vague address written on it. It had no house number, only a street name. But it was a good enough place to start.

"Alright, let's go and get him then," Avery said. "But let me phone Charles. Maybe he can meet us there or arrange for the police to get there before we do."

Her mother lifted the bag of books over her shoulder as Avery dialed Charles' number.

"Leave the books, Mom—Charles, hi," Avery greeted him. "Listen, I'm texting you an address for Carl. Well, it's a street name. We're worried about my father; his phone is off, and he was expected home hours ago."

As Avery talked, she gathered her car keys and unlocked the front door.

"Yes, we have the same concerns that you do," she continued. "Do you think you could—"

As Avery pulled the front door open, she saw her father standing there with his arm raised in the air, about to knock on her door. She felt dizzy with relief when she saw that he looked absolutely fine.

"Don't worry, Charles, my apologies; he's just arrived home. False alarm," she said before ending the call.

"Where were you off to?" her father asked. "I figured your mother would be here when I found the house empty."

"Dad, why aren't you answering your phone?" Avery snapped. "Mom's been worried sick about you. She thought you'd be home ages ago, and we were about to send the police to look for you!"

Her father shrugged. "My battery died, dear," he said. "I did send your mother a text to let her know that I'd be eating dinner at his house."

Avery turned to look at her mother, whose mouth was hanging slightly open.

"Well, I never received any message," her mother said.

Avery held out her hand. "Let me see your phone, Mom," she said.

There, as clear as day, was the notification that a message had come through a few hours before. She opened it, and it was from her father explaining that his battery was dying, that he'd be home late, and all was well.

She showed the message to her mother.

"Well, I didn't see it," her mother said plainly as if that made all their panic alright.

"Are you having tea?" her father asked between cheerful whistles. "Any chance I could get a cup?"

Chapter Seventeen

Her father walked right past them and made himself comfortable on the sofa. He had a wide smile on his face as he looked at the new décor in Avery's house.

"The books look lovely, dear," he said proudly. "I always forget how many of them there are."

"Thanks, Dad," Avery said, still dizzy from the stress that was leaving her body. "Tell me about your visit with Carl."

"Oh, it was just lovely to see him again," her father said. "He's doing so well, and we had so much to catch up on. That's the trick, isn't it? You avoid your friends for a few years, and then when you see them again, you actually have something new to talk about!"

Her father let out a child-like chuckle before leaning across the coffee table and taking Avery's cup of tea.

"Not at our age," her mother laughed. "If you wait too many years, your friends die, and it was all for nothing!"

"Everything was fine in the end!" her father said happily. "We spoke easily, and he was just as funny as I remember him to be."

"I told you everything would be fine," her mother said to him.

Avery couldn't believe it. Her mother had been the one who had started all the stress in the first place! She stared at her mother in disbelief, but she avoided complete eye contact with Avery. She sat down, her legs almost shaking from the brief panic she had just been through and leaned against the back of the armchair.

"What's even better is that I now know he is completely innocent!" her father said. "Just as I expected him to be."

"Oh, that's wonderful, dear!" her mother said, clasping her hands together with excitement.

Her mother carried on as if she hadn't just been on the verge of tears, convinced that her husband had been killed by a murderous lunatic. The entire thing had made Avery extremely tired, and she hoped her parents would finish their cups of tea soon so she could get into bed and forget that any of it had ever happened.

"Where was he then on the night of the wedding?" Avery asked, unamused by either of her parents.

Her father took a long sip of his tea as he lifted the ashtray on the side table, inspecting it.

"This was in your city house, wasn't it?" he asked. "I remember it used to sit on the table outside on the patio."

"That's right," Avery said, doing her best not to roll her eyes.

"He wasn't even in town," her father eventually explained. "In fact, he only returned to town yesterday. You should see his tan! He looks like he's just spent a month on a tropical island. He's been in Florida, enjoying the sun and the food if I looked at the size of his gut!"

Her mother gasped as if news of Carl's growing belly had been the most shocking part of the entire evening.

"Was he visiting someone there?" Avery asked. "Anyone that could provide an alibi?"

"That's the best part of all!" her father cheered. "He has just gone to see his children for the first time since they moved away. He hasn't seen them since they were young children."

"Isn't that wonderful?" her mother asked. "It must have been such a special moment. And I'm glad that his ex-wife finally let it happen."

"That's just the thing," her father explained. "His ex-wife wasn't too pleased about it, apparently. But his daughters are both adults now and live on their own, so they invited him to come and visit. And there was nothing that his ex-wife could do to stop it."

"It's a terrible thing to keep a father from seeing his children like that," her mother said. "I'm sure it must have meant the world to him to see them again."

Avery made a note of Carl's visit to Florida on one of the pieces of paper she had confiscated from her mother only a few minutes before. But she wasn't quite ready to drag a red pen line through his name yet.

"Apparently, those two daughters of his are quite the clever girls!" her father said. "One of them is an attorney of law, and the other just started her own business. He says he barely had to pay for a single thing while he was there."

"Do you think he could go live there with them?" her mother asked. "It's the least they could do for him after how he was treated by their mother."

"I wouldn't think so," her father explained. "Not so soon, anyway. He hasn't seen them in so long that he probably needs to get to know them all over again."

"I suppose that makes some sense," her mother agreed. "What a shame."

Her mother shook her head and tutted as she thought

about it. Avery looked at the clock and saw that it was well past ten and wondered how long it would take before her parents were too tired and agreed to go back home.

"I tell you what, though," her father continued at full steam ahead. "He's certainly improved his cooking skills since I last saw him. I had a really delicious meal!"

"Now I'm jealous that I didn't go along with you!" her mother teased.

"Not to worry," he answered. "I've taken the liberty of inviting him over for coffee next week. He said he remembers you fondly and was eager at the thought of seeing you again."

Avery was happy her father was so certain he was innocent because that narrowed their list of suspects down to one person. But she knew her father's claim regarding a conversation that nobody else had heard was not enough.

If they were going to convince the police that he wasn't involved, they would need a concrete alibi, something that proved his innocence without a shadow of a doubt.

"That's all lovely, Dad," Avery said with a somewhat forced smile. "You didn't perhaps get a contact number for one of his daughters or a photograph of the two of them together so that we can confirm his alibi?"

"How do you propose I could have worked that into the conversation?" her father asked with a frown.

"You never said anything about that when you asked your father to do it," her mother immediately joined in. "You just said that he had to make some light conversation."

"If you needed me to get those things for you, then you should have told me so," her father continued. "I didn't know that was necessary! I don't know how all these police things work!" Her father was waving his hands through the air, and Avery watched as a small drop of tea splashed out of his cup, landing all over his pants and the sofa beneath him. She had asked one question, and it had instantly upset both her parents.

"How, precisely, do you suppose it would seem normal for your father to ask his friend for a photograph to keep?" her mother continued. "You said he mustn't make himself suspicious! That would have sounded awfully suspicious to me!"

"Did you at least get a name for one of his daughters?" Avery asked.

"He mentioned their names a couple of times, but I wasn't paying enough attention. I'm an old man; I don't remember new names, only the old ones," her father answered.

"I'm sorry I asked," she said softly. "Just forget it. Thanks for going to see him, Dad. It was more helpful than you know."

Her parents finished their tea and with Avery's flashlight in their possession, they made the walk back to their home. Her mother's shoulder sagged under the weight of the books that she'd shopped for from Avery's bookshelf. Avery watched them until she couldn't see them anymore and then waited for the text from her mother to say they'd made it back in one piece.

Avery collapsed back into the armchair and reached for her notes. She stared at Carl's name with the red pen in her hand. But as much as she wanted to cross out his name, she couldn't yet. Her father had gotten some useful information, but there was no evidence to prove his claims.

Still, in her mind, Carl was no longer a suspect. So she wouldn't focus any more attention on pinning the crime on him. Beside his name she wrote the story her father had told her about how he hadn't seen his kids since his wife had left with them all those years ago. It was a good backstory, and she included a brief description of a large man with tanned skin and a love for cooking. And with that, one of the main characters of her book came to life. She wondered how many of James' characters had been modeled by people they had known personally.

Avery reached for the phone and dialed Charles' number.

"I'm really sorry about that; it was all a big miscommunication," Avery said when he answered.

"That's no problem," Charles said cheerfully. "It's always good news when a crisis turns out not to be a crisis at all."

"My father had been to dinner with Carl," Avery explained. "He was pretty casual about his choice of conversation, but he learned that Carl had been out of town in Florida. And if his story is true, then he only returned yesterday."

"How long was he gone?" Charles asked. Avery could hear him reach for a paper in the background.

"A few weeks at least, from what I can tell," Avery said. "He was staying with one of his daughters. My father didn't get any names or contact details, naturally."

"Oh, that's not a problem," Charles said. "I'm sure it won't be too hard for the officers at the station to get some information on his daughters. There should be contact information for them somewhere in the database. Or, at the very least, their mother could tell us."

"That's excellent," Avery said. "Will you let me know if you hear anything at all?"

"Tell you what," Charles said. "Why don't I pick you up tomorrow? We can go to the station and be there when they make the call."

"That sounds like a great idea," Avery said. "I can take some notes for my book. The more accurate, the better!"

"Great, I'll see you at ten then," he answered. "Now get some sleep."

"Don't mind if I do," Avery chuckled.

Avery took the entire stack of notes with her as she climbed into bed. She stared at the last remaining name on her list of suspects...Mrs. Scott. If the information they had was complete, then that made Mrs. Scott the murderer. She imagined the woman beating down the door and suffocating her own son. It just didn't seem to fit the appearance that Mrs. Scott liked to convey at all. She didn't seem right for the scene in any way. Or did she seem so wrong for it that it, in turn, made her perfect for it?

Avery wasn't sure she liked Mrs. Scott as the murderer, but she had a feeling that there would still be a lot that would come to light as the rest of the investigation continued. Her view of Mrs. Scott could still change completely, and she hoped it would.

She thought back to all of the books that James had written and tried to remember if, in any of them, the mother had been the murderer. There wasn't a single one. It had simply seemed too great a sin to write about, even in a crime novel.

Then again, few mothers were like Mrs. Scott, and few sons treated their mothers quite as badly as Dean had.

But there was one thing that didn't fit that potential storyline at all. Mrs. Scott would have no reason to break into her son's room. She was his mother, and if she had knocked, he would simply have let her in. Unless she had not done that on purpose to convince the police that the person who had done it had not been that close and friendly to him...

Chapter Eighteen

It was a warm morning when Charles picked her up. Avery was tired; she'd been up late working on some admin work for the vineyard. Everything at the vineyard was going smoothly, despite the fact that she was spending so much time away from it. It made her feel good to know it.

She was glad to see the cup of coffee waiting for her as she made herself comfortable in his passenger seat. She accepted it gladly and took a large gulp. She'd slept well the night before, but it had been so well that it had made her tired.

Avery had slept right through all of her alarms, including Sprinkles. And by the time she did wake up, she had to rush to be ready in time for Charles' arrival.

She had been in his car before and wondered why his car wasn't as cluttered as his home. If one had to judge him purely on the experience of his car, one might assume that his house was filled with clean lines and minimal furniture. There wasn't a speck of dust or dirt in his car, ever. In fact, Avery knew he had a habit of having it cleaned every week.

"Here," she said, handing Charles the beat-up cookbook from the bookstore. "I saw it, and it made me think of you."

The book landed heavily in his hand, some pages threatening to slip out and land softly on his lap. He pulled it closer and inspected the damage to the spine and cover and smiled. "Must be a good one, I guess," he teased. He paged through it and laughed. "Surely the pizza wasn't so terrible the other evening?"

"Not at all," she chuckled. "But your kitchen looked so sad and unused and lonely...just promise me you'll try at least one recipe out of the book?"

Charles leaned back and placed the book on the back seat. It was the ugliest item in his car, and the look of it kind of made Avery laugh.

"I'll make one," Charles agreed. "But you're going to have to come and taste it. I'll need an honest critique."

"Deal," she agreed. "I'll be as brutal as you need me to be."

At the station, Avery watched for what felt like hours as the officers made phone call after phone call. Eventually, they found someone who had been friends with Carl's daughter in school, and she had an old number for Carl's ex-wife. That number led them to one of her old friends, who had a forwarding address. Once they had that address, they could get his ex-wife's landline number. It took a few tries before she answered, but eventually, she was able to give them the contact numbers for both of his daughters.

She wondered how often they needed to go through such a lengthy process just to get the information that they needed. Carl knew his alibi would check out, and still, he refused to speak to the police when they had tried before.

That was a level of stubbornness that outmatched both

her parents combined. And in a way, she respected it. She wondered if it had made him a better cop and if that was why he had decided to continue to pursue the case against Dean, even when he was told he needed to stop.

She wondered if his stubbornness had been what had caused his wife to take their children and move all the way to Florida without him. Perhaps her mother had once contemplated the same.

It was finally time to phone his daughters. Everyone present gathered around the phone as it was placed on speaker. One officer was elected to speak, while everyone else was instructed to keep as quiet as possible and warned that the phone call was being recorded. They dialed the number for his eldest daughter, and it rang for what felt like minutes before the call ended without any answer. Then, they tried the number for his youngest daughter. Again, the phone rang and rang, and just when it looked as if that call would cut out too, there was a sound of a receiver on the other end as it clicked.

"Hello?"

"Hi, Miss Brown?" the officer answered.

"Speaking."

The officer went through all the formalities, explaining which precinct he was phoning from and even went as far as to give her his badge number for security purposes.

"Right," she said, sounding unamused. "I need to leave the house for a very important meeting. Is everything alright with my father?" She sounded nervous as if she was worried that she was about to receive some bad news.

"There's been a murder here, unfortunately. Your father is alright, but he is currently a suspect in the case. We're hoping you can confirm his alibi for us. Is it true that your father has been with you for the past few weeks?"

"That is correct," she answered hesitantly. "He spent two weeks here with me and two weeks with my sister, who I am certain would be happy to confirm."

"That's alright," the officer said. "Do you think you could both send us some photographs confirming the trip? Anything with a date stamp and a landmark in it should suffice."

His daughter happily agreed, and within minutes, an email had come through with photographs that proved his trip to Florida. They were happy photographs of a man in the sun, enjoying the day with his daughters. It was clear in the pictures how pleased Carl had been to reconnect with them.

Avery drew a red line through his name on her notes and then used the same red pen to circle the name of the remaining suspect.

"Our list of suspects is getting rather short now," Charles said out loud.

It wasn't her place to join in on the conversation. She was only a visitor in their investigation, and she'd been extra careful not to get too involved or to step on any toes while she had been there.

But she wished she could and knew that if she didn't concentrate hard on not talking, that the words would come falling out of her mouth and they wouldn't stop until she had said too much. She didn't want to do that. She wanted to keep the opportunity to follow them around. Avery wanted to write her book, and she wanted it to succeed. And for now, that meant biting her tongue and watching without inter-ference.

"Yes," the officer agreed. "Mrs. Scott is the only name left up on the board. And I really thought it would be Carl, I tell you."

Avery wondered what they would do next. Time was of

the essence, and there was a town full of people who needed answers. The talk in all the coffee shops was that people were afraid. One of the people among them was a murderer, and the reality of that was causing paranoia in the community. That was a dangerous place to be as a small town.

"I guess it is time we should bring her in," the officer said. "There's only so long we can wait out of courtesy. She is our only remaining suspect, and courtesy no longer matters."

The police officers in the room decided on their best approach. It was decided that the best option was to go and collect her and bring her in for questioning. It was the consensus that she was the kind of woman who would simply refuse to come in without her lawyer present. They hoped to speak with her for a while without his presence. Everybody knew who her family lawyer was, and he was a fierce practitioner of the law. He knew every loophole and had no problem suing anybody and any business on her behalf. And as long as there was money involved, she was happy to go forward with any suggestion he had to make.

Avery had met a few lawyers like that one when she lived in the city. She could spot them from a mile away. They always sported the finest watches and shoes. They walked in a certain way and spoke to everyone as if they were the smartest person on Earth. She tended to stay away from people like that for as long as she possibly could. And she knew well enough that if Mrs. Scott asked for her lawyer, it could mean trouble for the precinct.

The officers prepared themselves. Each one was given a different role to play. They had one chance to get her without her lawyer present, and they weren't prepared to miss that chance.

"Should we follow them?" Charles asked quietly, with a wide smile.

"Are we allowed?" Avery responded. "Won't they be upset with us if we do?"

"As long as we don't get in the way, and as long as we don't interfere, we are allowed to go wherever we please," he answered. "Provided we're not trespassing on private property, of course."

Avery knew most of Mrs. Scott's farm was open to the public. It meant they could drive onto her property, and legally, they were allowed to be there as long as they stayed off her private driveway.

She had nothing better to do at that moment, and she had been curious about Mrs. Scott and what she was like ever since Charles had added her name to their list of suspects. Avery wasn't going to pass up this opportunity.

"In that case," Avery said. "Of course, I want to follow them."

They followed as closely as they could in Charles' car, and Avery took note of every small detail. While she was in the car, she made a brief summary of the events of the day so she could use them accurately in her book.

Scott Rose Farm was titled proudly in brushed steel on the large gate as they entered the property. Every wall was white, and white roses stood proudly at the sides of the road. Avery looked out of her window and gasped quietly. It looked like something out of a book or a princess movie.

As far as the eye could see, there were roses of every color and every shape. On a different day, she would have loved to go out and touch them and smell them. She wondered if Mrs. Scott ever got tired of the scent of the roses around her.

I never get tired of the smell of wine.

When they finally came to a stop, there was already a police officer telling Mrs. Scott that she needed to go with him. Her house, painted bright white, was tucked away between the roses, almost invisible from a distance. And Avery had to squint to see her.

One thing was for certain; it was one of the most impressive farms Avery had ever seen. She wondered why Dean would ever have considered selling it. Who wouldn't want a place that beautiful?

"What is this about?" Mrs. Scott asked sternly.

As usual, she was dressed in all white. Her lips were red, and her hair was done up the way it always was. She looked as if the farm had sculpted her, and she had been born from its very foundations. The white of her clothes was the exact white of the walls and the surrounding roses.

"Some new information has come about regarding your son's case," the officer said. "We'd like you to come to the station so that we can discuss it."

Mrs. Scott looked skeptical, and Avery couldn't help but think that her skepticism made her seem guilty. But the officer just remained as calm as he could be, and he remained friendly with her, and eventually, she was convinced.

"Good job," Charles said quietly.

They watched as Mrs. Scott climbed into the back of one of the police cars, her lips pursed and her arms folded. One thing was for certain—she wasn't happy. Surely a mother would be happy to hear that there was some movement on the investigation into her own son's death?

To Mrs. Scott, the entire thing just seemed like one great inconvenience.

"Where will they take her?" Avery asked. "To a cell?"

"No, she has to be under arrest for that," Charles answered. "She'll be taken to a room for questioning. There'll be cameras and microphones. I expect she will lawyer up as soon as she sees the room."

Charles was right. When they made it back to the station,

Mrs. Scott had been placed into one of their interrogation rooms. She looked entirely out of place against the gray concrete walls and the gray table and chairs in the room with her. The room was small, but the emptiness made it seem as if it loomed over her head.

They watched on a sea of television screens as she checked her watch and rolled her eyes. She tapped her foot impatiently as if there was perhaps somewhere more important she needed to be at that moment.

"Odd behavior," Avery said. "If it had been family of mine, I'd be willing to wait as long as necessary to know how the case was going."

"You're absolutely right," Charles said. "And these moments are precisely why we make them wait. It's important to see how a suspect behaves without an officer present. She looks calm, frustrated, and impatient even."

"So what does that mean?" Avery asked.

"That means that should they ask her a question, and she suddenly bursts into tears and becomes distraught, that all of that is likely an act."

"I see."

"If she were going to cry and grieve, she would be doing it now in this brief moment of silence that she has to herself," he continued. "People who have lost loved ones to murder find it hard to maintain their composure in a room like that. The police station is a horrible reminder to them of the truth."

"What if they're just trying to be brave?" she asked.

"Nobody puts on a brave face when they think they're alone," he said, pointing at the screen. "If this were normal, she'd be a lot more heartbroken than she appears to be right now."

An officer that Avery didn't recognize joined them as they

watched the screens closely for signs and clues in her body language.

"Are you sure these are all recording?" Charles asked. "This is great body language to use in your case against her."

"Yeah," the officer answered. "And we're just preparing to start the questioning. We won't let her stew for too long, and we don't want her getting nervous and calling a lawyer."

"That sounds smart."

"Do you think I would be allowed to watch the questioning?" Avery asked, her eyes glued on the screen as she scribbled down notes.

The officer looked at Charles. "Is she a consultant like you?" he asked.

"She's writing a book," Charles explained. "Chief Mathers agreed to let her follow the case for some inspiration and research."

"I see, well, I'd have to run it past Chief Mathers, and I don't want to waste too much time," the officer said.

"Not to worry," Chief Mathers' voice answered from behind them. He stood beside them and faced the screen. "She can watch," he said. "Take her to the viewing room. I'll be there in a minute too. I'd like to see this one myself."

"Thank you," Avery said with a curt nod.

"Just don't cause any trouble for me," Chief Mathers said. "Women like that will take any reason to make my life hell. I can't afford that; my health is bad enough as it is already."

"You have my word."

Avery followed the officer down a few narrow passageways until he opened a door for her. And there she was, just on the other side of the glass. Mrs. Scott was staring at her own appearance in what she thought was a mirror.

But to Avery, it looked as if she was staring directly at her.

Chapter Nineteen

Chief Mathers joined Avery and Charles in the small viewing room. "Right," he said, clasping his hands together. "A few rules for you, Avery."

"I'm listening," she said, her eyes still fixated on Mrs. Scott.

The light hanging above her had made her look even paler, and all her white clothes seemed to glow. She looked ethereal, and she sat dead still, staring straight ahead. Avery wondered how she managed to remain so calm through all of this.

She looked particularly at peace for a woman who had just lost her son and had just been taken from her home to sit in a cold room and wait for ages for anyone to even explain to her what she was doing there. If Avery had been in her shoes, she might not have been able to sit so still. Even as she watched, she felt so excited that she was shifting uncomfortably on the spot.

"You can take notes, but you cannot use actual quotes," he said. "And you certainly can't use anybody's real names. I am doing this to help you with your book. I ask that you are respectful of my rules. None of what is said inside here can leave this room. The police force can face some serious consequences."

"I understand," Avery said with a kind smile.

She knew that Mrs. Scott had enough money to open a lawsuit against the department, just as her son had done when he ended Carl's career. Avery reached for her notebook and pencil and waited eagerly for the questioning to start.

Chief Mathers eventually left them, and Avery waited a few seconds before the door opened into the little gray room, and he stepped inside. He was colder than she expected him to be. He greeted her with a short "Mrs. Scott" and a polite nod.

He sat at the table across from her. Avery watched as he moved in his seat over and over again, as if he was finding it impossible to get comfortable. The chair creaked and squeaked, and eventually, he sat still and sighed. Then, he opened the folder in front of him and arranged and rearranged the pages inside over and over. From where Avery was standing, it seemed to be entirely without purpose. He sprawled the pages out in front of him before stacking them up again.

After that, he took his pen and pretended to read through some of the sentences here and there on the pages. Avery kept her eyes on Mrs. Scott, whose pout was becoming more and more pronounced. At that point, Chief Mathers took out a clean piece of paper and tested his pen on every corner, even though it wrote perfectly fine. Charles let out a short chuckle next to her as she watched what she felt was a ridiculous way to start any kind of interview.

Finally, Chief Mathers seemed ready to start questioning,

and he leaned forward on his elbows, looking up at Mrs. Scott for the first time since he had entered the room. What he met was a death stare that could end the world.

"Ah," he said, getting up from his seat. "I forgot my coffee."

After all of that shuffling and fiddling, he walked right out of the room with the folder under his arm, leaving Mrs. Scott alone in there again. Mrs. Scott rubbed her temples and let out an exasperated sigh. At that point, the door opened again to the viewing room, and Chief Mathers walked in and stood next to Avery.

"What was all that about?" Avery asked.

"I'm just trying to frustrate her a little," Chief Mathers explained. "I do think I'm getting somewhere, don't you, Charles?"

Charles snorted. "I think so, yes."

"Why are you trying to frustrate her if you want her to work with you?" Avery asked. "You need her to be forthcoming, not furious!"

"Well, in my experience, people who are calm keep a level head and lie better," Chief Mathers said. "But people who are angry and stressed will snap. And what follows that is usually some kind of rage-fueled confession."

"He's right," Charles said. "I used to use this method all the time when I was still on the force."

Avery wondered what a woman like Mrs. Scott would be like if she was pushed to the point of explosion. *Is that what happened when she killed her own son?*

"I'd like to get to the bottom of this, and she is a tough lady," Chief Mathers said. "So, hopefully, this helps."

Chief Mathers then left the room again, and what felt like minutes later, the door opened, and he rejoined Mrs. Scott without any coffee in hand. "I got all the way there and realized I don't actually want any coffee right now," he said with a casual chuckle.

"Excellent," Mrs. Scott deadpanned.

Avery made a note of Chief Mathers' tactic to get her to snap. It was an interesting one that Avery was certain would work on her. But at that point, it was clear that Chief Mathers couldn't waste any more time.

"Your full name and surname, please," Chief Mathers said with a pen in hand.

"Please tell me you're kidding," Mrs. Scott said. "You've known me for years, Adrian."

"It's a formality," Chief Mathers answered. "Your full name and surname, please."

Avery found it almost comical as Chief Mathers asked her a string of questions that he almost certainly had all the answers to already. With each answer that Mrs. Scott was expected to give, the less patience she had with him.

"I think it's working," Avery said quietly.

"I have to admit," Charles chuckled. "He sure knows how to frustrate a woman, doesn't he?"

Although Mrs. Scott's face seemed unchanged and stern, from where Avery and Charles were standing, they could see her fiddling with her hands beneath the table. Avery made sure to note everything about her body language, slowly creating a new character for her book.

"I'm sorry, Adrian," Mrs. Scott eventually interrupted him. "What exactly is it that I'm doing here? If this is all you need from me, we really could have done this from the comfort of my own home."

Mrs. Scott trailed the gray walls with her eyes, giving every inch of the room a disapproving look.

"Well," Chief Mathers sighed. "I should probably tell you

that you're a suspect in this case, Mrs. Scott." Her mouth fell open as he finished his sentence. She looked as if she had seen a ghost, and unbelievably, her face became even paler. Mrs. Scott swallowed hard.

"That's preposterous," she said softly. "I thought you had brought me here to tell me that you'd finally caught the person who has done this."

"We've brought you in for questioning," Chief Mathers confessed.

"Why is he telling her?" Avery asked. "He shouldn't have told her yet. He was really getting somewhere earlier."

"He has to tell her," Charles explained. "She asked him, and he cannot take her from her home and bring her here without reason."

Avery scribbled that down in her notebook and turned her attention back to Mrs. Scott and Chief Mathers.

"How dare you," Mrs. Scott said through gritted teeth.

"Well, she snapped," Avery deduced loudly. "Perhaps we'll get a confession out of her after all."

"We have reason to believe you might be the murderer here," Chief Mathers continued. "We know you've been angry at him. He wanted to move you and sell some of the heirloom buildings. We know he wanted to sell the farm."

It looked as if a fire had ignited in her eyes at the mention of her farm being sold. And for the first time since they had put her in that room, she showed some kind of emotion. But it wasn't remorse or grief. It was pure anger.

"We might not have been on good terms. That is no secret," she said. "But that does not mean that I have murdered him."

"Look, I know this is tough because my mother is your friend," Chief Mathers said kindly. "But I need to solve this case, and if you're a suspect, then you will be treated just like every other suspect."

"It's those other suspects you should be talking to right now," she barked.

"They've all been cleared, I'm afraid," Chief Mathers said, leaning back with his hands comfortably behind his head. "You're the only suspect left on our list."

"I might have joked about killing him or threatened to do so while we were fighting," she said with a massive frown. "But that doesn't mean I'd actually do it. It's insane for you to believe that!"

Mrs. Scott's foot was tapping impatiently against the concrete floor. She looked as if she wanted to reach out and slap the chief of police right across the face.

"You're supposed to be protecting our citizens," she snarled. "Not wasting taxpayers' money on this kind of nonsense."

"Questioning a suspect is not nonsense, in my opinion," Chief Mathers said. "And I am sure the rest of the town would agree."

"Well, get on with it, then, so you can see that I am innocent and take me back home," she said impatiently. "Then you can get back to work trying to catch the real murderer."

"She's awfully defensive," Avery said quietly.

"Mrs. Scott, where were you on the night of the murder at around ten o'clock?" Chief Mathers asked.

"I had dropped Dean off at his guest house, and then I drove home," she answered. "I offered for him to stay with me, but he said he'd rather die than do that. I suppose he sealed his own fate, then."

Avery was appalled at her lack of emotion toward the death of her own son. She understood how the other people in town might not have liked him. But it really takes a lot to get a mother to not like her own child.

"Was there someone with you?" Chief Mathers asked. "Or someone who saw you arrive home and can confirm that time for us?"

"You mean someone that can confirm my alibi?" Mrs. Scott mockingly asked. "No, I drove home alone that night and walked into my house alone. It's one of the many symptoms of being a widow."

"Well, we can't just take your word for it," Chief Mathers said. "Without evidence that those were your actual whereabouts, you will have to remain a suspect in this case."

The questioning was nothing like it was in the movies. They didn't throw images of the crime scene across the table at her, and there was no spotlight shining in her eyes. The police chief wasn't smoking heavily. It was clean, cold, and to the point.

Mrs. Scott was a small, petite woman who somehow had the ability to make herself seem like a giant with just the tilt of her head. She peered at Chief Mathers down the length of her nose and stared at him for a while.

"If I am your only suspect at the moment, then I fear for the safety of our town," she said. "Because that means that our police force is truly incapable."

"I don't think that's accurate," Chief Mathers argued. "This might not have gone the way you would have liked, but we have followed procedure, and we have taken someone we believe to be potentially dangerous off the street." He paused for a moment and shrugged. "And today, that person is you."

Mrs. Scott gasped. "I've never been more insulted in my life," she said. "Just wait until the news hears about this."

"I'm not here to flatter you, Mrs. Scott," Chief Mathers

said. "I am here to catch a murderer. And right now, that murderer might be you."

At that point, Mrs. Scott shut off entirely. She closed her mouth, and it quickly became clear that she had no intention of opening it again any time soon.

Chapter Twenty

Chief Mathers dropped his shoulders. From where Avery was standing, it looked as if he knew he had pushed her too far. Her lips were sealed, and that was the end of it. Mrs. Scott folded her arms and turned her eyes away from him.

Chief Mathers folded his arms, too, mirroring Mrs. Scott's every change in demeanor.

"When she moves, so does he," Avery whispered. "Why?"

"It's a technique that Chief Mathers always uses," Charles explained. "He mimics her. It's in an effort to relate to her. It's a complicated theory, but it works...puts them at ease, and eventually, they talk more."

But Mrs. Scott wasn't saying a single word.

Avery still couldn't understand it. All of this should have devastated her. She should have cried, pleaded, and had angry outbursts. She was angry, yes, but it wasn't exactly an outburst. As far as it was all concerned, she seemed too calm for what would have made sense to Avery.

It looked like a dismal scene. The overhead lights had started to flicker, and there was a prolonged silence. It carried on so long that Mrs. Scott eventually started to check on the condition of her nails.

"I'm giving you a chance to come clean before this goes too far," Chief Mathers said, his confidence breaking slightly.

In the darkness of the viewing room, Avery held her breath. She felt so tense about the situation; it felt as if they had been moments away from the entire murder being solved, but they missed it.

"We've lost her," Charles said quietly. "She's closed up and won't talk again, that's for sure."

"How can she be so calm?" Avery asked.

"I don't think she is," Charles chuckled. "She might look calm, but I think she is holding back and maintaining her façade."

"Her son was murdered, and they're accusing her of doing it. How can she keep this up?"

Chief Mathers sighed and shuffled some of the pages around as loudly as he could. He was still trying to get her to snap.

"You know I wouldn't have brought you here if I didn't think there was some gravity to this," Chief Mathers said sternly.

Mrs. Scott barely blinked. She didn't even turn her head.

"In that case, I won't speak again until my lawyer is present," she said coldly.

A coded knock at the door got Chief Mather's attention. He looked toward it as if he was waiting to hear another knock, and that knock would come. He clenched his jaw, frustrated immensely by the interruption.

"If you'll excuse me, it seems that my attention is needed elsewhere for a moment," he said as he gathered his papers together. "I assure you, I will be back here as soon as I possibly can."

"And I hope that my lawyer will be with you when you get back," Mrs. Scott responded.

Chief Mathers scratched his head in defeat and exited the room. Avery expected him to step back into the room with the suspect within a matter of moments, but that never happened. Instead, the door to the viewing room opened, and in walked Chief Mathers along with another police officer she didn't recognize.

"This better have been a good interruption," Chief Mathers barked.

The officer reached into his bag and pulled out a file. "I have the results of the autopsy of Dean Scott."

Chief Mathers paled and took the folder from him, flipping open the cover of it. His hands paged through it all as he read the information before him. He nodded and sighed as he paged through each page, paying careful attention to each detail.

"What does any of this even mean?" he eventually grumbled.

The officer took the folder back from him and tried his hardest not to roll his eyes. He pulled out a single page with some information listed on it.

"This is the only page that really matters," the officer said. He pointed to a line on the page. "It seems that the alcohol levels in his system were ridiculously high."

Chief Mathers looked back toward Mrs. Scott. "She said she drove him home but never mentioned he was intoxicated. When we'd questioned her initially, on the night of the murder, she said he seemed to be rather tired. She didn't say that he was drunk."

"And that would be because of this," the officer said, pointing to another piece of information on the page. "It shows that he had a lethal dose of Alprazolam in him."

"Alprazolam? And what might that be?" Chief Mathers pressed.

"It's a medication prescribed to handle high stress and anxiety," the officer answered. "It appears that this is the cause of death."

"Not suffocation?" Chief Mathers asked.

"There seems to be no evidence of suffocation on his body," the officer said.

Chief Mathers closed his eyes and ran his fingers through his hair. The tension levels in the room were so high that Avery felt the hair on the back of her neck stand up. She knew this information would change everything. It was the perfect plot twist.

"We have to rethink everything now," Chief Mathers said, looking toward Mrs. Scott. "When the method changes, so does how we look at our suspects."

"That medication could have been given to him at any time. It means that the suspect wouldn't even have had to leave the wedding to murder him," Charles said. "They'd have to be there to steal the money but not to administer the medication."

Avery couldn't even make any more notes for her book. She watched as each person in the room started to show signs of nervousness.

"Go in there and ask her if her son was on any kind of medication for stress," Charles suggested.

And they watched as Chief Mathers did just that. But he got no response at all. She remained silent, with her lips sealed shut as tight as they could be.

"I guess we're really not getting anything more out of her, are we?" Chief Mathers said when he returned.

"These things happen, Chief," Charles said calmly. "Just gotta keep pressing on. At some point, the evidence will point in the right direction. Until then, keep asking questions and keep finding answers."

But the chief of police was in no mood for any kind of advice.

"Thank you for reminding me how to do my job," he answered sarcastically.

Avery didn't care about the sarcasm and the tension in the air at all. In fact, she had practically stopped listening. Her mind was flooded with thoughts and questions. She went over everything she knew about Dean in her mind as she tried to piece together the events of that night.

Then, she reached for her copy of the diary entry that the police had read out loud that night. She read it again for what felt like the hundredth time.

I came back here to see the friends and family that I have missed. But I've only been met with unfriendliness and disgust. Threats have been made to my life, and it seems that nobody is on my side anymore.

It is clear to me now that some of the people on the guest list for tonight would love nothing more than to see me dead. But they simply don't understand me. And that is their own loss.

This time, as she read it, it seemed entirely different to her. The voice in her mind that spoke as she read the words sounded different. His diary was such a personal thing to him. Could it be possible that it was the only place in his life where he showed any sincerity?

If that was the case, then the diary entry meant something entirely different from what any of them had initially thought.

Avery tugged on Charles' shirt and motioned for him to follow her outside.

"What's up; are you okay?" he asked with concern.

"I'm alright. It's just...read this note again, with the information that we have now," Avery said.

Charles took the page from her and read it silently. But she saw the look in his eyes and knew that he saw it differently, too. He read it again and gazed upward, his eyes fixed on the wall behind her.

"What are you thinking?" he asked.

"I don't think he wrote this in the way we initially thought," she explained. "I don't think this points the finger at the guests of the wedding, or anybody else, for that matter."

Charles thought about it for a moment. "Does it then hold no significance at all?" he asked.

"Knowing what we know now about the Alprazolam, I think he took all those pills himself," she said.

"That's an interesting thing to say. What makes you think that?" he asked.

"He was a narcissist," she explained. "And although it is unlikely for narcissists to take their own lives, they might do it with the sole purpose of hurting someone."

"That's a bit of a stretch," he said, but she knew he was thinking it over a little more.

"If he really had been under severe stress, enough to need medication...who knows how that might have affected his ability to think straight after all that alcohol?" she asked. "Perhaps it was just a bad cocktail, and his mind got the better of him."

"What about the missing satchel of money?" he asked.

Avery shrugged. "It's missing," she said. "But we don't have proof that it was stolen. He was drunk and highly medicated. He could have done anything with that money, for all we know."

"You might be onto something," Charles said. "I mean, nobody at the wedding wanted him there, and he would have known that. Alcohol and medication might have blown the situation well out of proportion in his mind."

"He's so narcissistic that he might have done it out of spite," Avery said.

"And in that state, with all of that in his bloodstream, it is entirely possible that he broke his own door down," Charles continued. "He might not have intended to do it. If the door was already loose and he lost his footing, it might have been easy enough."

"He would have opened his own safe," Avery added. "And who knows what he did with the money in that deluded state?"

Charles read through the diary entry again and raised his eyebrows. "This isn't the whole thing. This is only the part that they felt fit for the public to see. Wait here."

He disappeared down the hallway for a bit and returned with a paper in hand. "Here's the rest of it," he said.

I came back here to see the friends and family that I have missed. But I've only been met with unfriendliness and disgust. Threats have been made to my life, and it seems that nobody is on my side anymore.

It is clear to me now that some of the people on the guest list for tonight would love nothing more than to see me dead. But they simply don't understand me. And that is their own loss.

My mother doesn't want to move. And they don't want me to sell the building. The bookshop wants to stay where it is.

Multiple people tonight have told me to pay back the money to Deb. I can't think straight anymore.

Perhaps it is time to give them all what they want.

"Why didn't they want us to see this?" Avery asked. "Why was this not part of what they read?"

"They didn't want people to automatically point fingers at the people mentioned. And they figured he had just decided to do what was right. Nobody thought that the last line referred to his death," Charles explained.

Avery stared at the diary entry and noticed that the rest of what was written was barely legible. She ran her fingers over the badly scribbled words.

"This must have been once the medication and alcohol had taken full effect," she said.

"Maybe he took all the Alprazolam on purpose," Charles said. "We need to tell Chief Mathers."

Avery and Charles entered the viewing room, where the discussion was still ongoing. Chief Mathers was asking the officer with the autopsy report a string of questions about the medication and some details about the autopsy.

"Excuse me, Chief," Charles said. "But we have something we'd like to run by you."

"Are you sure it's important?" Chief Mathers said, unimpressed. "I'm kind of in the middle of something right now."

Charles looked him dead in the eyes. "We think he killed himself."

Chapter Twenty-One

C hief Mathers and the other officer stared at them with their mouths hanging open. It took them a few seconds before either of them could find something to say.

"That's a rather bold statement," Chief Mathers said bluntly. "What makes you so convinced?"

"This is really Avery's theory, so I'll let her talk you through it," Charles said, stepping aside.

Her stomach sank to the bottom of her feet, and she swallowed hard. She felt like a girl in school, expected to give her presentation to the class. Avery had never been comfortable with that kind of thing, and immediately her fingers started toying nervously with the seam of her shirt.

"It's the rest of the letter," she said, holding it out to Chief Mathers. "I think he medicated himself and overdosed. And as Charles has theorized, he might have broken the door down himself in his intoxicated state."

She stepped further into the room so she could speak more directly to Chief Mathers. "I know there is missing money," she said. "And that does seem odd. But there really is no evidence that it had been stolen."

A vein appeared across Chief Mathers' head, and it was as if Avery could witness the headache forming beyond his skull. A frown broke across his face as he sighed.

"Well, you make a compelling argument. Thank you," he said, sounding rather ungrateful if Avery was honest.

"It's a lot more work for us to look into," he continued. "But I'd like to make sure that we're positive suicide isn't an option before we continue looking at it as a murder."

"Are you sure?" the other officer asked.

"Unfortunately, yes," Chief Mathers answered. "Looking at the note now, it is entirely possible that he did this to himself. I don't want to waste our time any further if that's the truth."

Avery wasn't sure if she should be proud or apologetic. She was pleased that she had pieced it all together but had completely disrupted their process. And none of the officers involved seemed pleased about it.

"I want you to go through all of his belongings again," Chief Mathers instructed the officer. "Look for prescriptions, receipts, or bottles...anything that can prove the medication was his. In the meantime, I'll try to find out who his doctors were."

The officer glanced over at the interrogation room. "What will we do about her?" he asked.

Chief Mathers sighed and looked at her for a while. "Well, we can't really question her anymore," he said. "We'll have to let her come in with her lawyer. I think I've pushed her too much already. We can't face another lawsuit from the Scotts."

Avery didn't like that. She had hoped to see some more drama from Mrs. Scott. What she had seen wasn't nearly enough for her book. She had hardly anything to work with yet. But what she did get was an idea of the process, and that was better than nothing.

Chief Mathers exited the viewing room, and a few moments later, he appeared in the interrogation room. His shoulders were hardly as squared as they were when he had first entered, and his hands were empty of any folders.

"Mrs. Scott, you are free to leave whenever you please... unless you'd like to talk," he said.

She didn't say another word. She stood up, fixed her hair, and walked toward the door. But Chief Mathers stopped her before she left.

"I will need you to be back here next week, and you can bring your lawyer. We still have a lot of questions for you," he said.

"A week?" she scoffed. "I won't be dealing with this for a week. I'll be back here tomorrow. Don't waste my time again."

The sound of Mrs. Scott's footsteps echoed past them as she walked through the halls and toward the exit. She kept her head up, proud, but the slight twitch in her lip was a faint sign that she had been embarrassed.

"I assume someone will be driving me home?" she called loudly.

A nearby officer jumped up to be of assistance, and she dumped her white bag into his hands. He followed her as if he was her personal chauffeur. Avery had never seen such an impressive display of confidence and wondered if it would work for her, too, or if she first needed a couple million dollars.

"Right," Chief Mathers said. "I have a lot of paperwork to do after all of that, and my officers have some evidence to comb through. Avery and Charles, you two are welcome to stay, but who knows how you'll keep yourselves busy here. That's it for now." With that, he spun on his feet and left them behind. The other officer walked calmly in the direction of the evidence room.

"So, now what?" Avery asked.

Charles shrugged. "A few steps back in this investigation, unfortunately. But for now, I'll wait to hear more, and I'll let you know."

"Do you think they'll let me come back tomorrow for the questioning with Mrs. Scott?" she asked.

"It's tough to say," he answered. "Everything is a little different when the lawyers get involved. But let me see what I can arrange."

Charles and Avery walked through the police station, and around them, officers worked tediously at heaps of paperwork. Phones rang constantly, and the faint smell of coffee lingered permanently in the air.

They'd spent so much time in the viewing room that when they finally stepped outside, the bright sun blinded them. The day was already in full swing in town. Coffee shops were full, and people filled the streets. The weather was good, and everyone seemed happy.

But all Avery wanted was another cup of coffee.

"Shall we get back?" Charles asked, holding the door open for her.

It seemed like a foolish question. They had nowhere else to be, and if he had been asking her to go somewhere else, he had a funny way of doing it.

"I guess," Avery chuckled.

Avery enjoyed driving with Charles. It was nice not to be in control for a while, and she easily trusted him with her life.

"How do you know all that stuff about narcissists?" he asked.

"James wrote a book once where the main character was a narcissist," she explained. "I know it seems crazy to base all my theories on a book character, but there was extensive research done."

"Is that so?" he asked. "Well, it's paying off."

"Yeah, James and I went to talks and read books about narcissists in order for him to craft the perfect character. It's amazing how clear they become once you know what to look for," she said.

"Yeah?" Charles asked. "I didn't realize there was a blue-print for people like Dean."

"Well, there is one book that came close to being just that," Avery said. "Sydney Koh wrote a book called *Dealing with the Unavoidable Narcissist in Your Life*. That book alone shaped the entire character that James had written."

"It sounds like you were pretty involved in those books," Charles said. "More than you like to let on."

"Well, one thing you don't understand about writers is that their work becomes their life," she said. "And not in a bad way. They're creative people, and they can't help it. And I wanted to spend as much time with him as possible. Thankfully for me, it was kind of fun."

Charles laughed. "And you learned a lot too! I'm sure it was an interesting way to live. It paid off. I've read his books. All that work was certainly worth it."

"Thanks," she said bashfully.

"So, how did that book end?"

Charles looked at her, and he had a childlike smile on his face. He seemed completely interested, and Avery wasn't used to it. Most people tried not to talk to her about her husband too often or for too long. It made them worry that she might be sad or it would ruin her day.

But Charles didn't mind it so much. He seemed adamant that Avery remembered the good times that she used to have with her husband. And she appreciated him for that. In the process, he got to know her better.

"Well," she chuckled. "The narcissist had taken some medication in an effort to get some attention. She only wanted to be hospitalized. But it went wrong."

Charles raised his eyebrows.

"She took too much and died accidentally," Avery continued. "In the end, there was no murderer."

"I see now how you pieced everything together back there, then," he said. "Do you think Dean Scott could have done the same?"

"I don't know," she said. "But his diary entry does seem a little odd. And there were people making his life difficult. It had crossed my mind that he hid his money to make it look like a robbery."

"It seems like a silly way to go," Charles said. "Accidentally killing oneself. And it seems like a lot of work just to get back at someone."

"Not when you're a narcissist," Avery explained. "People like that are always thinking of themselves. They are the center of the universe, and they refuse to believe that their idea might be a bad one. Some of them might truly believe that they are above the laws of nature. And those who are unfortunate enough to get close to them rarely make it out undamaged."

They pulled back into the driveway at Charles' house. Just seeing his house made Avery smile as she remembered the pleasant experience she'd had there when they enjoyed pizza and wine.

"Thank you for your help," he said as he opened her door for her. "And I am glad we were able to clear Carl's name. None of that could have been done without your help."

"It's really no problem at all," Avery said. "My father had

a great time talking with his friend. I believe he will be going back to visit soon. It's just a pity we didn't get more out of Mrs. Scott."

"Well, how about we have some lunch and talk more about this suicide possibility?" he offered.

Avery looked back at his house. She thought about his antique glasses and the endless heaps of books. She wanted so badly to go inside and have a look at his treasure chest of a house. She thought about the good wine that she had there the last time and how he had made her laugh. She wished she could accept his offer. But she couldn't.

"I'm expected at a wine tasting with the girls," she said, a little disappointed.

"Ah," he said. "Stammtisch?"

He acted casual, but Avery noticed a slightly disappointed slump in his shoulders. He tucked his hands into his pants and swayed slightly, looking out over the mountains in the distance.

"As always," Avery laughed. "But perhaps we can have lunch here soon? I need a new book to read, and you have an impressive collection."

"Alright," Charles agreed. "But how about next time you come, I make you one of those pizzas? I can't promise that it will be edible, but I can promise that I will put my best effort into it."

"That sounds like a great idea," Avery laughed. "I'll bring the wine."

Charles gave her a hug. They didn't hug often, but this time felt a little different. Charles wrapped his arms tightly around her and lingered just a little longer than she was used to. It felt good to be comforted—it was a feeling that Avery hadn't felt in quite some time. Charles was warm and comfortable, and he was familiar to her. And when she left, she felt sad to be leaving him behind. They'd spent the entire morning together, and she still wanted to spend more time with him.

She enjoyed his company, his conversation, and she felt warmer after she had been with him. She watched him grow smaller in her rearview mirror as she gave him one final wave goodbye. And he watched her leave until she was out of his sight.

Chapter Twenty-Two

The wine-tasting room was large, with glass walls and ceilings. Avery felt small inside the giant glasshouse as she sipped on the wine. The views surrounding the farm were some of the most beautiful that Avery had ever seen. Outside, Sprinkles enjoyed the fountain along with some other dogs who had accompanied their owners for the day.

Rolling hills were on display in every direction, and large trees cast shade under which families held picnics and fed the birds. Inside the glass house were easily a hundred plants, creating a wild, tropical paradise for those eager to sample some of the vineyard's best wines.

All the women of the Stammtisch, excluding Eleanor, sipped happily at their wine. And the more they sipped, the more they laughed. Glasses clinked, and chatter filled the air as they caught up on everything they had missed since they had last seen each other.

They usually saw each other often enough that there wasn't all that much to catch up on. And Avery had become grateful for their gatherings. They'd been a healthy distraction from her busy work life and a pleasant change from her quiet personal life. They made her feel less lonely. Without them and Charles, all she would have was her work at the vineyard and Sprinkles.

So, even if she had heard the same story thousands of times, she listened happily, eager for them to fill some of the quieter moments in her life.

When they'd sampled a little too much of what the vineyard had to offer, they went for a walk to cool their cheeks and work through some of the alcohol. It was a pleasant day, and it was a beautiful place for a walk.

Small footpaths circled various gardens on the property, showing them only the prettiest views and spaces that the vineyard had to offer, and for a brief period, the women could pretend that they were far away from their town and somewhere new entirely.

"Thank you for all your help getting me removed as a suspect," Deb said cheerfully. "It really means a lot to me."

Avery wasn't entirely sure how to respond. With the new information on how Dean had really died, she couldn't be certain that they wouldn't put her back on the suspect list. After all, it was entirely plausible that Deb had placed the medication in his drink while they were at the wedding.

Deb did seem to Avery like the type of person who might take such medication. She had been through a lot of stress and behaved like someone who experienced a fair amount of anxiety. But that was merely speculation, and Avery didn't want to linger too long on that thought.

"It's really no problem," Avery said. "We had to do something...it was getting ridiculous! And the rest of the bunch helped a great deal. They provided so many photographs and videos."

"It was your idea, though," Deb said, nudging her. "And it was a genius one! What did their faces look like when you showed the pictures to them? I hope they were irritated like they had irritated me."

Sprinkles barked playfully at a passing butterfly and bounced after it, stumbling over a nearby twig. But he was barely on the ground before he was up and running cheerfully back to Avery's side.

Avery wasn't entirely sure what to say to Deb. In the end, the officers had moved on so quickly after removing Deb from the suspect list it was hard to believe they ever cared about it at all. So, she had no answer for Deb's question.

Instead, she just said, "I'm really sorry you ever had to go through any of that...the whole suspect-in-a-murder-thing but also everything Dean put you through. It's rather pathetic if you ask me."

Deb shrugged. "I should have known that it wouldn't end well. There were so many signs that should have told me how unimportant I was to Dean."

It was a terrible thing to say, and Avery felt bad just hearing it from her.

"I guess not entirely unimportant," Deb chuckled. "I gave him a place to live—not that he needed it."

"It's easy to see those things once you're through it. When we reflect, it all seems so much clearer than when it was staring us in the face," Avery commented.

"It should have been more obvious to me, though," Deb said. "Our relationship was all about him. And there were days when I was so aware of it. But if he bought me even one bunch of flowers, I would just forget it all and convince myself somehow that I was happy."

"We can convince ourselves of many strange truths if they have a pretty enough face," Avery said. "You can hang artwork over a hole and, in a matter of seconds, forget that the hole had ever been there, to begin with."

Deb nodded. "He had this way of making me feel as though he cared about me and what I was doing," she said. "He always told me how he wanted me to be successful and wanted to see me at my full potential."

She sighed and stopped to inspect a leaf of a nearby tree. "But he actually wanted my success for himself. He knew that the more I made, the bigger our house could be. None of it was because he cared. He had an image to maintain, and he wanted to make sure that I could fit the description."

"Well, I am sure that, in reality, you were too good for him, anyway," Avery said, placing a comforting hand on Deb's shoulder.

"And in the end, there had never been anyone that was good enough for him," Deb continued. "If my information is correct, I was the longest relationship he ever had, and no girl-friends after me ever really stuck."

"Can you blame them?" Avery laughed as she took a stick from Sprinkles' mouth, tossing it for him to run after.

"It made me feel foolish in the first few years after we split," Deb said. "How had it been so clear to the women who had followed, and yet I had been so blind to it all?"

"Don't beat yourself up about that," Avery advised. "There's no point to it anymore. You've moved on just fine after him, and that's all that matters."

"He left me and went to the city when he felt that I hadn't been successful enough for him," Deb explained. "That's what it said in his notes. He said he was going out to find someone who really understood him and what he needed from life."

Avery had never heard of anything so hurtful. She imagined how she might have felt if someone had said or done those things to her. And even in her imagination, it stung more than a hot blade through her chest.

"That's terrible," Avery whispered.

Deb nodded. "And he felt that I owed him for all of his wasted time. He said it was because he was putting so much work into me that he hadn't had the time to collect the furniture he needed for his own home in the city."

"It seems like an absurd notion," Avery said. "But to a man like that, it must have made perfect sense. Men like Dean believe the entire world owes them something...gratitude for their very existence. They show up and believe their presence has changed the world. It's ridiculous."

"Well, he certainly changed my world when the bill arrived for my credit card," Deb said. "I'd never been so heartbroken in my life before."

Avery could see the heartbreak on Deb's face and knew that it still hurt her.

"He set me back by years," Deb said. "By the time he left, I had worked hard for everything that I owned, and I had to sell almost all of it. I had no money to spend on anything other than my bills for years. And in the meantime, he lived happily in the city, carefree and in his own world."

"It's hard to believe that there was nothing that could be done about it," Avery said.

"Well, I gave him my credit card with permission once to go and buy some groceries for me. It was one stupid mistake. Because of that one time, he was able to spend my money and get away with it," she said. "And by the time I learned about it, it was way too late."

"I can't imagine how devastating that must have been," Avery said. She wasn't entirely sure what Deb wanted or expected her to say. It was a terrible story, but Avery realized Deb simply wanted to get it all off her chest. Dean's death would have been a painful reminder to her of what he had done.

"He had the money to buy those items," Deb said. "He was rich, and so was his family. But that didn't matter to him. According to him, the energy that he supposedly put into me was worth something. He had billed me for his time."

"Did you really never get back any of the money?" Avery asked.

Deb shook her head. "No, he never sent me back a cent. In fact, he never spoke to me directly again. Every correspondence I received from him after he left was in the form of a formal letter from his attorney."

"Was he really that much of a chicken?" Avery asked. "Too afraid to speak to you?"

"I don't entirely blame him," Deb chuckled. "After I had first received the bill for my credit card, I kind of went off the rails a little. I said some terribly hurtful things to him and about him. After that, he refused to ever speak to me again."

"Did he speak to you at the wedding?" Avery asked.

"Of course not," Deb said. "He stayed as far away from me as possible. Everybody there knew what he had done to me. He was probably concerned about what they might say if we were seen standing so near to each other."

"Why do you think he went to the wedding at all?" Avery asked. "You heard what he wrote in his diary. He knew nobody wanted him there and that everybody hated him, and still he went."

"Attention," Deb said with a scoff. "It had to have been for the attention. It didn't matter to him if everyone hated him. Even if the attention he was getting was bad, he was eager for it. As long as his name was on everyone's lips, he didn't really mind what they were saying."

"Well, he might have slowed you down a little, but he certainly didn't hold you back," Avery said. "Look at you now. You are more successful than he ever was, and you got there with honesty. And everybody loves you. You were better off without him."

"That's for sure," Deb agreed. "I hate to think of what my life might have been like if he had stayed. If I had married Dean, I don't think I would ever have truly been happy."

Deb reached for a flower and plucked it, tugging lightly at the petals as she inspected them closely. "It took me many years to trust anybody again after Dean left," Deb said. "I really had never expected it from him, and it shattered me. Still, I am careful with new people. But after all this time, nobody has ever hurt me like that again. So, I suppose it's time to let it go."

Avery wondered if she would ever feel comfortable enough to move on from James. She wasn't entirely certain she had the courage to do it. It was not easy to put trust in another person like that, and she had spent so much of her life with James that she wouldn't even know where to begin with someone new.

She missed her husband. There was a space that he had always occupied, and a silence that he had always filled. But the thought of him no longer pained her. Avery knew she would never stop missing him or grieving for him. But she was grateful that the hurt she felt after his death had finally started to subside.

Chapter Twenty-Three

When Avery woke up the next morning, she knew Sprinkles was too restless for his own good. He got so excited to see her that he bounced around on the lawn with his ears flapping around, slapping him in the face. She needed to get rid of some of his energy, so she called him to join her for a walk. It was time for her to take a look at some of the vines at the edge of the property, and she figured that this was a perfect opportunity. He walked eagerly at her side as she picked a different route for that day. She walked all the way to the end of the property, past her parents' house, and along the perimeter fence.

There were some trees there that provided some much-needed shade for them as they walked in the morning sun. The bugs and the birds were coming to life as they moved, and bees buzzed past her, happily going about their daily business.

The vines looked healthy, and it made Avery feel proud. She wondered if Mrs. Scott got the same feeling when she walked through the endless rows of roses on her farm.

Sprinkles stopped to admire every bird that sang and

nipped happily at the butterflies that flew past. He was growing into his ears and his paws, and that only made him quicker and more agile as he playfully chased the beetles that zoomed past him.

Avery's eyes were still puffy as she tried to wake up, and her cup of coffee warmed the palm of her hand, creating a soft cloud of steam as she walked in the crisp morning air. The only thing she was missing was her sunglasses which sat waiting for her on a table right by the front door, with the plan that she would never forget them again.

She was deep in thought about the nature around her when she heard footsteps approaching. A small amount of city instinct kicked in, and she spun around, anticipating an unfriendly figure sneaking up on her.

Instead, she was met with the friendly face of her mother, who was out of breath from walking fast enough to catch up with them.

"I thought it was you that walked past earlier," her mother said.

"You thought?" Avery answered. "But you weren't sure. What would you have done if you marched all the way up here and I was somebody else?"

Her mother shrugged. "I would have wished them good morning and gone back to bed." She smiled. "Good morning."

Her mother attempted to give a sleepy smile back, her eyes puffy. One thing that Avery and her mother had in common was that neither of them were morning people at all.

"I forgot my sunglasses," her mother said, squinting into the sun as she approached Avery's side.

They walked together for a short distance, but Avery knew something was on her mother's mind. The only time her mother was that quiet was when she was trying to find the right words to say, which meant that she hadn't come out there just to make casual conversation.

"Everything alright, Mom?" Avery asked as she sipped her coffee. "You're awfully quiet this morning."

Her mother glanced back at the cottage she shared with Avery's father. "Your father has sent me to apologize," she said bluntly.

Avery chuckled. "What does he want you to apologize for?"

"For the other night," her mother said. "I shouldn't have walked without my flashlight, and I caused you stress. I'm sorry. I just—I can't get the hang of these silly cellphone things. I missed his text, and it caused a fair amount of upset, and I feel terrible about it." Avery had already forgotten all about that ordeal, and the thought that it had bothered her parents so much was all that worried her now.

"It's alright, Mom," Avery said. "You did the right thing. You thought he was in trouble, and you came to me. You'll know better to check your texts next time," Avery said.

Her mother shrugged. "We'll see," she said ominously.

"I'm sorry too," Avery said softly. "I didn't mean for Dad to be so stressed before meeting with Carl. I hadn't considered that it might make him so anxious. I never wanted him to feel that way."

"We know that," her mother said. "I shouldn't have gotten so upset with you about it. He's a grown man; if he didn't want to go, he should have just canceled."

"When has Dad ever canceled plans?" Avery joked. "He's got commitment issues, but not the usual kind. He commits too seriously and then never goes back on his word, even if it means trouble for him."

"You're right!" her mother laughed. "Like that time he nearly got his nose pierced because of a dare. Thank goodness the piercing place was closed that day, and I had a little extra time to talk some sense into him."

Avery laughed at the memory and the mental image of her elderly father walking around with a pierced nose.

"Still," her mother continued. "As we get older, your father and I feel more and more foolish. We get so worked up about things that are really not such a big deal. We forget that everything is easier these days."

"It's okay, Mom," Avery said. "I understand that well enough. I am sorry I argued with you the other night about everything. I was just worried about Dad, that's all."

"Well, I put you there, so if you argued with me, I deserved it," her mother commented. "Maybe you should just come and show me how to do the stuff on the cellphone again." Avery shuddered at the thought. She'd spent countless hours with her mother, talking through every step of the process. If it were going to work, it would have.

"I tell you what," Avery said. "Why don't you and Dad just agree to stick to phone calls only? No more texting."

"That does sound a little simpler," her mother said. "That's the part I know how to do. It works just like the old phones. Punch in the number and dial 'em up! I don't understand why we ever needed to change that system."

Avery considered how significantly more complicated her life would be if she never had a cell phone to do her daily tasks. Although she had a memory of a time before cell phones, it seemed so distant and foreign to her. She no longer remembered what it felt like not to be so connected to the outside world.

"Hello, little one," her mother greeted Sprinkles.

Sprinkles had come to sniff her mother's shoes and legs and licked her hand to wish her good morning. He had a wide smile on his face as her mother ruffled the fur on his head, his ears swinging at the sides of his face.

He'd always liked Avery's mother. She had a tendency to sneak him treats when he wasn't allowed, and Avery wondered if she didn't perhaps have some in her pockets. Her suspicions were confirmed when her mother stuck her fingers into her pockets and retrieved a small dog biscuit, happily giving it to Sprinkles to enjoy.

"You can't keep doing that, Mom," Avery said. "How many times do I have to tell you? He is going to training lessons. If you give him a treat now, you are teaching him bad manners. I can't allow that." She had told her mother that countless times and her mother had never verbally responded. That silence was her mother's way of letting her know that she wouldn't listen and would continue to give the dog treats if she so pleased.

"How is it going with his training, anyway?" her mother asked.

Avery held out her hand, and her mother retrieved the rest of the dog treats, handing them over to her. Then, she called Sprinkles over to perform a demonstration.

Sprinkles performed flawlessly. He rolled, sat, and shook Avery's hand. Then, she showed how she could walk and keep him at her side, showing him when to change sides. Sprinkles showed Avery's mother how he could come to a complete stop or break out into a full sprint at the mention of a single word.

"Impressive!" her mother said with a wide smile.

"Yeah, we've been working really hard," Avery said. "So quit it with sneaking him treats."

"He's such a sweet dog! I can't help it," her mother said. "And so well-behaved—that training is really paying off."

"Not all the time," Avery said. "He did something so odd at the bookstore the other day."

"With Simon?" her mother asked, as if there could be any other bookstore that Avery was talking about.

"Yes," Avery sighed. "He begged Simon for his sandwich; can you believe it?"

"Sounds perfectly normal for a dog if you ask me," her mother said.

"Not for Sprinkles," Avery said. "I've been very strict in teaching him not to beg. And he hasn't begged for food in months, and then not again since that day. And none of my attempts to get him to leave Simon alone worked either."

"I'm sure it was just a moment of weakness," her mother said. "I wouldn't think about it too much."

"I wanted to ask the trainer about it the other day, but she was busy with another pet mom," Avery said. "Hopefully, I can catch her next time, and she can tell me what to do if that happens again. He needs to behave when we're in public."

"What kind of trainer is she?" her mother asked. "Is she one of those friendly folk who always speaks in a high-pitched voice the moment an animal comes near?"

Avery shook her head. "Nope, she used to train dogs in the military. She's strict, rigid, and ruthless when it comes to her training."

"Military?" her mother said. "That seems rather rough, doesn't it? Why would you need to train a dog that way?"

"Sprinkles loves it," Avery said with a smile. "He runs around smiling when he's there. She's strict, but she's still friendly. He's learning a lot that I think he wouldn't learn at any other training school."

"I've never heard of such a thing in my life," her mother said.

"Have you ever had a dog?"

"No," her mother laughed. "But I always wanted one. Your father wouldn't let me. He said I'd wind up loving the dog more and kick him out!"

"Well, Sprinkles does occupy most of the other half of my bed," Avery chuckled.

"So, is he learning anything in this special military training that he can't learn at any other training school?" her mother asked.

Avery nodded, swallowing the last sip of her coffee. "A few things, definitely. I've enrolled him in the advanced class," she explained. "I don't know if it will be entirely necessary, but he loves the classes, and it's a good release of energy for him."

"I see, so you take him there to tire him out a couple of days a week?"

"Mhmm," Avery answered. "And it's been great fun. Whenever he's done with training, he sleeps right through the night. I wish she would have a class on a Friday so I can sleep in a little on Saturday morning," she joked.

"So what kind of things has he learned in this special class?" her mother asked.

They watched as Sprinkles gleefully picked up a stick and brought it to Avery to throw. Naturally, she obliged and threw it as far as she could. Sprinkles raced after it, kicking up clouds of dust behind him as he ran.

"It's been pretty interesting," Avery said. "He has learned how to recognize and track smells, just like the police dogs do."

"Now, that is impressive," her mother said.

"It gets even better than that," Avery said. "He's learned how to be alert when someone nearby is showing signs of extreme distress. I'm not really sure how he knows, but Brie taught it to him, and I think it is pretty fascinating."

The sun was dappling through the leaves of the trees, creating a confetti effect on the ground as they walked. Her mother went quiet for a while as if the concept of a support dog had been completely foreign to her.

Avery wondered how her father would feel if she bought them a dog now. Would he still think it was a bad idea? Did her parents even have the energy left to care for another soul?

Her mother seemed to like Sprinkles a lot. And perhaps it would be a good incentive to get them out of the house to go for walks every day. Then again, it could backfire, and Avery would wind up caring for the dog for most of the time.

"So, what's the sign if someone is in distress?" her mother asked.

"Sprinkles will automatically try to comfort that person and stand at the person's side," Avery said. "It can be easy to miss, but it's meant to be subtle. If you know what you're looking for, it is easy enough to spot."

Suddenly, it dawned on Avery why Sprinkles had gone to Dean that day at the wedding.

Chapter Twenty-Four

Avery stopped dead in her tracks as she spoke the words. She had described what Sprinkles was doing when he stopped near Dean on the day of the wedding. He had been signaling that Dean was in distress, and Avery hadn't noticed. It made so much sense to her now. Sprinkles had pressed his nose into Dean's hand in an attempt to comfort him. But when Avery called him away, he happily answered. Avery felt dizzy as the realization hit her, and she immediately instructed her mother to turn around.

They walked as briskly as they could without risking her mother tumbling to the ground and breaking a limb. But Avery felt in a hurry to confirm her new theory. When they got back to her parent's cottage, her mother did her best to lure Avery in for a cup of coffee, but Avery managed to decline. It only took a few minutes of negotiation. And as Avery raced back to her own home to get ready for the day, she phoned Deb.

Deb had the footage from the wedding video, and Avery knew that there was no way the videographer missed the shot of Sprinkles walking down the aisle. She just had to get the right moment and watch it again to make sure she was right about it all. By the time she stepped out of the shower, Deb had sent the video.

Avery threw on some clothes, poured another cup of coffee, and played through the footage, waiting for the moment when Sprinkles stopped at Dean's side. When she watched it, she knew that she was absolutely correct.

"Clever dog," she whispered in Sprinkles' direction.

On the video, she could clearly see Sprinkles stop dead at Dean's side. He attempted to nuzzle into Dean's hand and get Dean to stroke him, but Dean wasn't interested at all. In fact, his hand seemed bizarrely unfeeling.

Avery messaged Charles to meet her at the police station and piled into her car. The traffic moved slower than she would have liked as people tried to get to work and drop their children off at school. Avery's finger tapped nervously against the steering wheel. By the time she got there, Charles was already waiting for her, and he had a cup of coffee in his hand.

"You're a blessing, do you know that?" she said as she gratefully accepted the coffee.

"You're welcome," he laughed. "Now, what's the hurry?"

"You'll see," she said as she rushed inside.

Chief Mathers watched through the footage as Avery pointed out what it was they were looking at. "I'm certain this is his signal to say that this person is in distress," Avery said. "I think Sprinkles stopped there because he could see that something was wrong with Dean."

There was silence as Chief Mathers scrubbed backward to watch the footage a few more times. "Is there someone that can confirm this?" he asked. "Who is the trainer for Sprinkles?"

"Brie," Avery said, pulling her phone out of her pocket to make the phone call.

Brie was confused when she arrived but no stranger to that kind of event. After all, she had trained dogs for the military and the police force. She just hadn't expected that kind of call to come from Avery.

Brie greeted everybody by name as she walked through the crowd of officers, and all the service dogs in the area came to greet her too. She knew the dogs all by name as well.

"What's this all about then?" she asked as she joined them in Chief Mathers' office.

Avery showed her the footage. "You trained Sprinkles to alert signs of distress in people, right?" she asked.

Brie nodded. "We've done a couple of classes like that, yes," Brie answered.

Avery pointed to the screen where the footage played. "What is Sprinkles doing here?"

Brie watched it once and smiled. "He's alerting to distress! I can't believe he picked it up so quickly! What a good boy! — Wait…isn't that the guy who was murdered?"

Brie looked up at Chief Mathers. "Yes," he answered. "This was taken just a few hours before he overdosed on Alprazolam."

"Well, he was in distress at the time that this video was taken," Brie said. "That is without a doubt."

"That means probably one of two things," Chief Mathers said with a sigh. "Either he was already contemplating the overdose, or he was already feeling the effects of it."

Brie raised her hands. "This is more than I should know," she said. "Is there anything else that you need me for?"

Chief Mathers smiled. "If you could just file an official statement before you leave to say that you've seen the footage and what your opinion is, that would be helpful."

"Of course," she agreed before leaving the office.

The doors to the police station flew open, and in marched

Mrs. Scott. At her side was a tall, lanky man with a briefcase. He was most likely her lawyer. He wore a large, expensive watch and crocodile skin shoes.

The two of them together looked like the type of people one would see on the front page, accompanied by a headline announcing their latest corporate scandal. She didn't stop to greet anyone. Mrs. Scott simply walked directly in the direction of the interrogation room that she'd been in the day before and waited impatiently at the door.

"I guess that's my cue," Chief Mathers said, rising from his seat. "Avery, you can watch if you like. Same rules as last time."

Avery waited for them to be in the interrogation room with the door closed before she stepped into the viewing room. Charles joined her again, and this time she knew that what she would learn would be of real importance.

"He's going to have to rethink his entire questioning strategy now, thanks to the new information," Charles said. "Good catch, by the way."

Avery smiled as she sipped her coffee which, at that point, had already gone cold.

"Mrs. Scott, there is something I would like to show you," Chief Mathers said, reaching for his phone.

He opened the video and played it for her a few times. It was the first time Avery had seen Mrs. Scott show any emotion. The footage of her son, taken just a few hours before his death, caused a slight wrinkle around her lips as the corners of her mouth became downturned. Finally, Avery thought she saw some signs of sadness in the stone-cold woman. There was something that made her human.

"That dog is alerting to signs of distress in your son," Chief Mathers explained, this time with a much kinder approach to the day before. "This footage has only recently been provided to me, and the woman who trained that dog has agreed this is his signal for distress."

Mrs. Scott watched the footage a few more times, her façade breaking more and more with each replay. Eventually, Chief Mathers put it away just as Avery thought she might see a tear from the victim's mother.

"We have reason to believe that Dean might have been struggling with his mental health," Chief Mathers said. "Do you know anything about that?"

Mrs. Scott looked toward her lawyer, who nodded to say that she could answer the question.

"Of course, he struggled with his mental health," she snapped. "How could he not after everything he has been through?"

Chief Mathers made himself comfortable in his chair. "I'm afraid I'm not entirely sure what you are referring to."

"Of course, you don't," Mrs. Scott answered. "Dean had a way of only ever showing the world what he wanted everyone to see. Behind closed doors, his life was completely different."

"Will you tell me what happened?" Chief Mathers asked.

Mrs. Scott again turned to her lawyer to get his approval before speaking. He nodded, and she turned her attention back to Chief Mathers.

"His business went under," she said plainly. "Just as I warned him it would. That's why he suddenly became so dead set on selling everything. He was drowning in debt and didn't want anybody to know about it."

Charles let out a disgruntled scoff. "I wonder if any of the money from those sales would have gone back to Deb."

"And I assume that he wasn't coping well with any of this?" Chief Mathers asked.

"Of course not," Mrs. Scott replied. "Everybody just assumed he was a monster, eager to ruin lives. In reality, he needed to sell the buildings to pay off his debt and attempt to save his business. And he was willing to do so at the expense of others."

"As far as the rest of us are concerned, his business has been thriving. He had made a point to tell us all that when we saw him just before the wedding," Chief Mathers said.

"Well, I suppose he was just trying to keep his reputation," Mrs. Scott said. "He stopped doing well after I cut him off financially."

Chief Mathers leaned back in his seat and seemed completely stunned. "I had no idea that he had no more access to your money," he said.

"That's because it isn't anybody else's business, now is it?" she retorted.

"She's got a point there," Avery mumbled.

"May I ask why you decided to cut him off?" the chief asked. "Even when he was struggling so badly financially?"

Mrs. Scott looked to her lawyer, again and again, he nodded. Avery wondered what his purpose was there that day. He seemed to be alright with every one of Chief Mather's questions.

"If you must know," she said, "I cut him off because he was blowing all my money on his gambling habit. I couldn't do it anymore. It was too risky. So, I cut him off. All he had was his business and the buildings that were in his name. Of course, at that time, I didn't know he'd already run his business into the ground."

Chief Mathers wrote it all down, making markings on the parts that were of particular importance to him.

"Had he ever mentioned to you about going on any medications to help with stress or anxiety?" Chief Mathers asked.

"No, he didn't," she answered. "We didn't talk much

anymore after I stopped him from losing my money. There has been little love between us over the last few years."

It seemed like an absolutely absurd thing for a mother to say about her son. But they were no ordinary family. It was quickly becoming apparent to Avery that the Scotts revolved their entire lives around money, and to them, money mattered more than anything else. Even family.

"When we spoke to you the night of the murder, you stated that there was nothing out of the ordinary when it came to Dean's behavior," Chief Mathers said. "But our autopsy results show he had a very high alcohol level. Why did you not mention to us that he had been drunk?"

Her lawyer opened his mouth to stop her from talking, but she ignored him. A frown broke across her face as if the question had insulted her.

"It has been a long time since I've seen my son sober," she said. "If he was drunk, then he wasn't acting out of the ordinary. That's been normal for him for the longest time now, so I doubt I would even have noticed." She paused for a moment and blinked away some tears. "If he'd been sober, I might have thought he was acting strange. Now, that would have been something worth mentioning."

Finally, Mrs. Scott showed signs of mourning. But she didn't mourn for the son who had died a few days before. She mourned for the son that she'd had years ago—the one that she'd lost to gambling and alcohol.

By the time it was all over, Avery felt completely defeated by it all. She slumped into her car and pulled the door closed. She had no idea how to feel about any of it. She certainly hadn't expected to become quite so invested in it all. By the time she left, they were no longer getting any information from Mrs. Scott. Her lawyer had finally intervened and put an end to it.

There was still a lot that the police needed to learn before the case was solved. They had spoken about finding out which medications Dean had been on if any. And they wanted to conduct a search of his private home in the city.

It was looking more and more as if there had been no murder at all. It left Avery feeling conflicted. She wanted to go home, but her hands rested calmly on her lap, not reaching for the steering wheel. She stared ahead as she tried to imagine Dean's last moments and piece them together.

With this new theory, she had no book. There was no murder and no strong enough story. Something about Dean's truth didn't really seem like something she wanted to sell. Avery sighed, and in her mind, she attempted to close that chapter and tried to convince herself it was time to move on.

She drove home in silence, her heart feeling conflicted about the conclusion of the case. It wasn't closed yet, but it seemed as concluded as it could be. She thought about Mrs. Scott and her strange behavior about her son's death.

Avery didn't have children, but she couldn't imagine acting that calm if anybody close to her had died. Let alone a child. She had Sprinkles, and she couldn't even imagine how she would react if he had died. Then again, Sprinkles wasn't going to move her out of her home and try to sell her business.

When she got home, a cheerful-looking Sprinkles awaited her. Avery knelt down to greet him, and he ran into her arms. She held him close, hoping that he'd simply live forever. It had been an intense day, so Avery was desperate to do something else and clear her head.

Chapter Twenty-Five

Avery waited outside her beloved bookstore for Charles and her father to join her. The sun was warm, and the town was bustling. As she waited, she watched the people around her and let her mind drift. When Charles finally greeted her, she jumped in surprise.

"Didn't mean to startle you," he said with a chuckle.

"That's alright; I wasn't paying attention," she said sheepishly. "I was too busy watching the world go by."

Sprinkles wagged his tail in excitement as Charles bent down to greet him but quickly abandoned him when Avery's father arrived. And as usual, Sprinkles went right to his pocket, and her father retrieved the treat.

"Dad," Avery sighed. "Please, I have asked you so many times not to do that!"

Her father signed to Sprinkles to keep quiet, winked, and didn't respond to Avery at all. Within a few moments, the group was inside and browsing the books. But Sprinkles was ill-behaved, just as before. He tugged at his leash, whining at the feet of Simon, who was trying desperately to mind his own business.

"See, Dad?" Avery said. "You're teaching him to beg for treats. All those hours at training are for nothing if you keep doing that."

"Nonsense," her father said. "He's not begging. He's on the hunt!"

"I'm afraid you might be right," Simon laughed as he produced a handful of treats.

She was about to argue with them both when Charles motioned to her to step to one side with him. She knew him well enough to know that the look in his eyes was one of concern. Avery handed the leash to her father and followed Charles to the other side of the store.

"He's not begging," Charles said quietly.

"He's not on the hunt either," Avery said, frustrated that nobody seemed to care.

"No," Charles said urgently. "Look at him carefully. It's like in the footage from the wedding. He's alerting."

Avery looked up, and from a distance, she saw it. Sprinkles wasn't whining at Simon; he was alerting to something else entirely. His tail wasn't wagging, and he was focused on only one spot below the counter. "What if that's just where the treats are?" Avery asked, but she knew it was a foolish question.

She knew that Sprinkles didn't beg. And as she looked at her puppy now, she knew that he was alerting to something— it just wasn't clear what, or why.

She tugged on Charles' sleeve, and he followed her back to where Sprinkles and her dad were. "Thanks, Dad," she said as she took the leash back from her father. "Simon, are you feeling alright?"

Simon looked uneasily at her and smiled. "Better than ever," he answered. "Today isn't as bad as it could be."

"Are you sure?" she asked.

"Are you okay?" Simon asked hesitantly.

The three of them had been looking at him. Avery and Charles were watching him closely for signs of distress, and her father had no idea what was going on. But he was eager to be part of the conversation anyway.

"Of course," Avery said.

Avery let go of the leash. She wanted to see where Sprinkles would go. And when he ran behind the counter, she and Charles took a step closer. Sprinkles had his nose pressed against a wooden box that was tucked away beneath the counter.

In an instant, Simon's demeanor changed.

"Hey, get your dog out from behind here!" he shouted. "If you're going to bring him in here, you better keep him well-behaved."

"What's in the box?" Charles asked.

"His treats, obviously," Simon answered.

"No," Avery said calmly. "You have treats in your hand. If he were after the treats, then he would have gone for the ones in your hand."

"Just out of interest sake," Charles said, acting casually, "show us what's in the box."

"This is getting ridiculous," Simon said, getting to his feet. "And it is a massive invasion of my privacy."

It had seemed that they were at a loss, and they really had no way of forcing him to open the box. But Sprinkles wasn't confined to the same rules that humans were. He bumped the box with his nose and let out a short bark to get their attention.

The box crashed to the ground and burst open. Dean's satchel came tumbling out, and the money fluttered to the ground, spreading all around Simon's feet. Before Avery and Charles could react appropriately, Simon had run for the door. But he was met by Avery's father, who stood in front of the closed door.

"Get out of my way," Simon growled. "Or I'll make you move."

"I don't think you will," her father said calmly, gesturing at Simon's shaking hand.

Simon looked around and knew that he was outnumbered. From where he had stood moments before, Sprinkles smiled proudly.

Within minutes, Chief Mathers was there, and Simon was being led away in handcuffs. It felt strange to see him that way. But the man he had become when they had questioned him about the box was not the friendly store owner she had known for so many years.

Avery's father was sent home with Sprinkles as Avery and Charles followed the police back to the station. Their statements would be necessary. And there was no way that Avery was going to miss the questioning.

It took longer than she would have liked to answer the police's questions about what had happened at the bookstore, and once she made it into the viewing room, the process was already well underway. But to her surprise, Simon was leaning casually back in his chair with his shaking hands resting on his knees.

He seemed friendly and unafraid, and once again, the reaction of the suspect made no sense to her. Had James had it wrong in all his books? Had they portrayed murderers in the entirely wrong way for all those years? She was looking at a criminal investigation for real now, and she saw no nervous jitters or angry outbursts. All she had seen were confident suspects that were unconcerned about their futures.

Simon smiled as he answered the questions and cracked jokes with the police officer.

"I tell you, Chief," he laughed. "I was just as surprised to see that money there as the rest of them were!"

"Then why'd you try to run?" Chief Mathers asked, unamused.

"I was coming to get you!" Simon explained. "The moment I saw that cash settling around my feet, I knew I had been set up."

"If that's the case, then why did you refuse to open the box?" Chief Mathers asked.

Simon shrugged. "It wasn't mine to open," he explained. "I didn't know whose it was, so I couldn't go and open it, now could I?"

Chief Mathers sighed. "This doesn't look good, Simon, and it doesn't make any sense either."

"Look at me!" Simon argued, holding his shaking hands out in front of him. "I can barely hold a cup of water! How am I supposed to murder anyone?"

Avery was holding her breath and hadn't realized it until she felt a wave of dizziness wash over her. She leaned on Charles to keep herself upright, and he didn't seem to mind.

"You alright?" he asked quietly.

"Yeah," she said. "Just a bit nervous."

"I'm afraid this might not go the way you think," Charles said. "They might have a motive, but they have no evidence that he actually killed the man. All they have is possible theft. And, I hate to say it, but he could be telling the truth."

"He ran," Avery said shortly.

"I know," Charles said. "But without proof that he had the means to do the murder, we can't pin it on him."

Avery's mind was swimming with frustrated thoughts and unanswered questions, and she didn't want to deal with it for a moment longer. She had an idea, but she just needed help from someone she could trust who wouldn't ask any questions.

"Wait here," she instructed Charles. "I'll be back. Don't leave until I'm back."

"Avery?" she heard him ask as she closed the door behind her.

Chapter Twenty-Six

"I'm here," Tiffany said, out of breath. "I came as soon as I could. I told everyone at work I had an upset stomach. What's so important?"

"I knew I could trust you," Avery said with a smile.

To Avery's surprise, the bookstore was still open. Behind the counter, she spotted a man that looked like a younger version of Simon. It had to be his son. It occurred to Avery that times must have been really tough for his family if they couldn't even close the shop for one afternoon while his father was being arrested.

It almost made her rethink the entire idea. But then she remembered Dean and how he had died. She turned to Tiffany and walked her through the plan, and just as Avery had anticipated, Tiffany happily agreed.

Tiffany walked into the building first. Her only task was to distract Simon's son long enough to get him up the stairs. Avery waited outside and peered through the window, waiting to see their two pairs of feet as they moved up the spiral staircase.

But Tiffany played her role even better than Avery could have ever expected.

A high-pitched scream came from the upstairs floor of the bookstore.

"A rat!" Tiffany screamed. "There's a great big rat!"

Simon's son went hurtling up the stairs to tend to the damsel in distress, and Avery took her shot. She moved in as fast as she could, going straight behind the counter and into the room where the kitchen was. She searched through the shelves as quickly as she could. She was looking for something specific.

Her hands fumbled at every bottle and jar that she could find, but she didn't find it. Then, she searched behind the counter, beneath the cash register. There she mostly found notebooks, stamps, and pens. She could hear Simon's son's voice getting louder.

"I don't see anything, ma'am," he said. "I suppose you'll have to let me know if you spot it again."

Then she heard the first of his steps at the top of the staircase. Avery was running out of time, and she knew it. But as she glanced up, her eyes caught sight of a small zipped-up bag on top of a pile of books to the side of the counter. On it was a label with the word medicine printed on it. She reached for it and stuffed it under her shirt, making it out of the door just in time to not be spotted. It wasn't clear yet if she had found what she was looking for, but she had done the best that she could.

Tiffany followed her act through to the end. "Well, thanks," she said as she walked toward the door of the bookstore. "I'll be back again once you've dealt with all the rats in here." Tiffany beamed with pride as she walked back onto the street. She looked as if she'd had way too much fun.

"Did you get it?" she asked eagerly.

"I hope so," Avery said. "You did a great job, by the way."

"Thanks," Tiffany said proudly. "We should do that more often."

Avery had no time to waste. She drove back to the police station, and as soon as she arrived there, she asked for a pair of gloves. With the gloves secured over her hands, she searched through the contents of the bag, looking for what she was certain she would find. When she did find it, it took every ounce of her self-control not to jump up and down and cheer. But her excitement was short-lived. Because on the bottle of pills was the name Simon Simmons. The officer behind her went deadly silent, and there was a soft exhale.

"He's going to want to see this," he said.

He pulled on some gloves and reached out his hand. Avery placed the bottle in his hands and followed him down the hall and back into the viewing room.

"What did I miss?" Avery asked as she joined Charles at his side again.

"Not that much," he said. "He says he didn't do it, but they still think he might have. I really don't know what to think. Where'd you go?"

"You'll see," she said with a small smile.

The door to the interrogation room opened, breaking the solid gray of the wall only momentarily. The officer who had just been with Avery stepped inside, and it was clear to everyone by the look on his face that his interruption was important.

The officer leaned down to whisper in Chief Mather's ear before handing him the bottle of pills. Avery watched Simon's face closely, and as he watched the handover happen, he lost all the color in his face. His casual demeanor changed, and his eyes darkened.

He looked to Avery like someone who knew he'd been caught.

"Simon," Chief Mathers sighed. "I really think it would be best if you just came clean."

Chief Mathers slid the bottle of pills across the table. In large blue letters, it was labeled, Alprazolam.

"Where did that come from?" Charles said seriously.

"From a little bag on the bookshelf of his shop," Avery said.

"How did you get it?" he asked, turning to her in disbelief.

"I'll tell you about it later," she said hurriedly. "Do you think he'll confess?"

Simon looked at the bottle, which clearly had his name on it, and shrugged. "Not entirely sure what this is supposed to mean," he said, doing a terrible job of pretending that he didn't care.

"This," Chief Mathers said, tapping the top of the bottle, "is the medication that we know murdered Dean Scott."

"That's ridiculous," Simon said. "Do you know how many people take that medication? Me and anybody else with stress and anxiety. It's not that rare."

"Well, piece it together with the discovery of the missing satchel in your possession," Chief Mathers explained, "and I can't help but think you're the one who murdered him."

"I have no reason to have murdered him," Simon said. His arguments were only becoming more and more feeble. His shirt was slowly darkening with sweat, and the shaking in his hands was getting worse.

"Of course you do," Chief Mathers said. "You stood to lose your business if he sold that building, and that reality was only weeks away."

Simon remained quiet. He took a deep breath and stared

at Chief Mathers with angry eyes. Avery wondered what his plan was. Did he think he could intimidate Chief Mathers into dropping the accusation?

"Oh, come on," Simon said. "Everybody in this town knows me. They'll all tell you that I could never do this."

"That doesn't matter if we have the evidence," Chief Mathers said.

With the adjustment of his shoulders, Avery knew that Chief Mathers was done arguing with Simon.

And his stare was enough to make Simon break. Simon's eyes filled with tears, and his shoulders dropped.

"I spoke to him at the wedding," he explained. "I wanted to know what he was going to do about the sale of the building."

"Go on," Chief Mathers said, writing it all down.

"I didn't want to do it, but I would lose everything if he sold that building," Simon continued. His eyes were downcast at his swollen hands, and Avery could see the shame that loomed over his head.

"I had hoped that he was going to say that he decided not to sell the building after all," Simon said. "If he'd just gone with that decision, I would never have slipped the Alprazolam into his drink."

"But that's not what he said, is it?" Chief Mathers asked.

Simon shook his head. "No," he said softly. "He said that the sale was due to go through any day now. I hated him for that so much. And in that moment, there was nothing I wouldn't do to change that reality."

"How did you get it into his drink?" Chief Mathers asked.

"I had it ready, just in case," Simon explained. "I had it crushed up and in a small pouch tucked into the cuff of my sleeve. I just pointed at a beautiful woman, and while he looked away, I slipped it into his wine."

Avery watched as he was read his rights and charged with the murder of Dean Scott. It was a crime that he very nearly got away with.

"Well done, Sprinkles," Charles said. "Remind me to get him some treats."

Simon was taken away in handcuffs as he requested his lawyer to be contacted, and Avery wondered if he thought it was worth it. Granted, his family could continue on with the business, but they would lose their father to prison.

Perhaps he really wasn't the man that the community had believed him to be.

Chapter Twenty-Seven

THREE MONTHS LATER...

Every paper and news program was filled with the news of Simon's sentencing. All the evidence had pointed against him, and in the end, it was easy for a jury to find him guilty. Avery had attended every one of his court dates, and she'd learned more than she could ever have imagined.

Simon would spend the rest of his life in jail and still awaited trial for many other crimes that had been uncovered during the investigation. Avery wasn't sure yet if the bookstore would survive it, but she had high hopes. There was no reason that a place so magical needed to suffer for the actions of one selfish man.

It had been a long trial. Simon had used his health to delay the court dates as much as he possibly could, making it a tedious and drawn-out experience.

Avery sipped her coffee victoriously as she saw the image of him behind bars on her television screen.

But by the time the sun was at its highest point in the sky, she had forgotten all about Simon. She joined the women of the Stammtisch as they gathered in the backyard, along with Avery's parents. Chief Mathers had promised he would make an appearance at some point as well. She wished Charles would be there, but he still needed to work in the wine room.

There had been a party tent set up, and there were treats and wine enough for the entire town, it seemed. The music was flowing, and it was the perfect day. Summer was coming to an end, but the sun was warm enough that day as if it had put on one final show for Avery and her celebration.

There were fresh flowers on the table, and the women had all color-coordinated their outfits. Bright colors made them look more festive than ever as they celebrated the release of Avery's first novel.

In the center of the table was a single copy on display. "The Bookshop Butcher" stood proudly for all to admire. And within a few days, copies would be available for purchase in almost every bookstore. It seemed unreal to Avery, but nobody else seemed quite as surprised.

"I've already read the book twice!" Deb bragged as she slid her chair nearer to Avery.

"Well, I started reading it, but I got too stressed out!" Camille commented.

Eleanor reached for the book at the center of the table and looked at it as if it was the first time she'd ever seen it. She admired the cover and read the description on the back, despite the fact that each person in attendance at the party had received a personalized copy in the mail weeks before.

They celebrated until the last bit of daylight disappeared behind the horizon. Avery enjoyed the celebration very much. It only made her want to do more things that were worthy of a celebration.

When Avery finally put on her pajamas and got ready to collapse onto the couch, the party décor was still outside. She was too tired to tidy it up yet and knew that it wasn't going anywhere. *I can do it tomorrow.*

She picked out a movie to watch and was about to press play when she heard a familiar knock at the door. Avery chuckled as she realized she had come to know Charles so well that she could recognize him by the way he always rapped three times against her door paused for a moment and then knocked one last time.

"You had to wait until I was in my pajamas, didn't you?" she said as she opened the door with a smile.

But Charles' face was obscured by a badly put-together cardboard box.

"I promised you I'd try it," he said as he handed it to her. "Besides, there was no way I was going to miss celebrating with you today."

Avery opened it, and inside was one of the worst-looking pizzas she had ever seen. She stared at it a moment, doing her best to keep a straight face, but it wasn't working.

"Oh," she said, flustered. "Well, you did your best, and that's all that matters."

Charles burst out laughing. "Luckily, I brought these along too!"

He revealed his other hand, and in it was a pizza box from the pizzeria down the road from him. And on top of the box sat two antique wine glasses with a ribbon tied around them.

"I saw these and thought of you," he said with a smile. "I know you've got the wine to fill them if you're interested?"

Avery and Charles celebrated on their own with pizza, wine, antique wine glasses, and a movie that neither of them had really seen before and neither of them really enjoyed, either. Thankfully, they had more than enough to talk about to drown it out.

The End.

~

Did you enjoy *Murder at the Vineyard Inn*?

If you loved this book, you'll definitely want to check out
Murder at the Cheese Shop!

Here's a sneak peek...

The peaceful atmosphere of Los Robles is shattered when a murder takes place at the neighborhood cheese shop, causing chaos among the tight-knit community.

This full-length whodunit will keep you guessing at every turn. Join Avery, Sprinkles, and the gang from Le Blanc Cellars for another adventure!

Turn the page to start the first chapter!

Murder at the Cheese Shop

SNEAK PEEK

The peaceful atmosphere of Los Robles is shattered when a murder takes place at the neighborhood cheese shop, causing chaos among the tight-knit community.

Local innkeeper and vineyard owner, Avery Parker, is shocked to discover that she is implicated in the mysterious death in her small hometown.

As Avery begins to investigate, she encounters a myriad of suspects, each with a convincing motive. She uncovers secrets and betrayals from past and present love interests, a disgruntled ex-employee, and a suspicious resident.

Her captivating journey leads her to hidden agendas in the search to solve the crime. The gossipy residents have their guesses, but who can she really trust?

With twists and turns at every corner, *Murder at the Cheese Shop* is a thrilling mystery that will keep sleuthing readers on the edge of their seats.

Wine pairings and irresistible recipes included!

Don't miss out on this thrilling mystery - order your copy today!

Visit https://a.co/d/hqMb0T6
to get *Murder at the Cheese Shop* now!

~

Chapter One

The cold morning air stung the tip of Avery's nose as she waited outside Cheesy Does It. She needed to buy some cheese for that evening's gathering of the Stammtisch. They were a group of women from Los Robles who got together informally to enjoy each other's company. And in that small, central region of California, the gatherings were becoming more and more frequent and that group of ladies was quickly becoming best friends.

But she was too early for the cheese shop that morning. She had been in such a rush to get there so she could buy cheese and get back to her vineyard to start the daily work that she didn't realize she had left way earlier than any of the shops on that stretch opened. Thankfully, there had been a coffee shop nearby that was serving.

So, she sipped the coffee, allowing the steam to defrost the tip of her nose while her golden retriever, Sprinkles, slept at her feet. It had been an earlier-than-usual morning for him too. That part of Los Robles was so quiet that morning that it felt as if she was the only person on the street.

When she answered a call from Charles, she felt as if her voice was the only thing that could be heard for miles, and she wondered if she'd be responsible for waking up everyone within walking distance of where she was standing.

She had gotten used to the small town. It had been a while since she'd moved from the city after her husband had died in a boating accident. She had been convinced that she would never recover from it. Yet, she had survived.

To her surprise, since she left the bustling city and moved to a smaller town, she had been busier than ever before. Apart from running her parents' vineyard, she had written and published many crime novels, a skill she had learned from her late husband.

She hadn't written nearly as many as he had in his career, but she had certainly adopted his passion for it. It filled her late, sleepless nights and gave her a creative outlet that she never knew she needed. With friends in the Stammtisch, a rewarding job, and a newfound creative passion, she was feeling more at home than she ever had before.

"Charles, it's way too cold out here," she said. "This cold has come earlier than I expected; I worry about the vines."

"What are you talking about?" Charles laughed on the other end of the call. "You've had a great few seasons! A bit of cold weather shouldn't scare you. Besides, there's always eiswein!"

"Oh, I don't know if those good seasons came because of me, or because of luck," she teased. "Honestly, there are some days where it feels like I have no idea what I'm doing."

"Well, you have a good way of hiding it," Charles answered. "You always look completely in control if you ask me. I think you're just tired, and it's making you feel worried about everything that didn't worry you before."

"If that's the case, then the good news is that I've run out of books to write."

Charles burst out laughing on the other end of the line.

"What do you mean?" he asked. "How can you run out of books to write? You only just got started."

"I don't know where James found all the inspiration," she said. "The first few I wrote were inspired by some of the old case files here in Los Robles. The police were kind enough to let me go through them."

"So, go through some more," Charles eagerly suggested.

"I've tried!" Avery argued. "There's nothing interesting anymore! There are only boring murders left. If there is such a thing."

"Boring?" Charles asked. "They're murders!"

"I know, I know, but you know what I mean," she said with a chuckle. "They're all the standard ones. You know, an angry wife catches her husband cheating... There's not much of a story there. Not one that I can work with, anyway."

"I can't believe you'd think any kind of murder is boring," Charles said.

"You were a police officer," Avery argued. "You see these things differently. I need a story to tell. I need something with twists and turns and drama. Most of the murderers here seem to turn themselves in. I can't work with that."

"I see," Charles said. "I get it, but it doesn't sound right when you say it was boring," he teased.

Sprinkles had startled awake after the first cyclist for the morning came zooming past them. Thanks to his training, Avery could keep him still with just the motion of her hand, which was difficult to do that morning considering her hands were currently full.

She was starting to understand why some of the younger people around her opted for headphones and earbuds to talk to their friends. She quite liked the idea of hands-free calling. Especially when she was talking to Charles, as their conversations tended to go on for quite some time.

"Tell you what," he said. "When you come over to my house tomorrow, we can go through some of those so-called boring case files, and we can think of ways to make them more interesting. You just need a little inspiration, that's all."

"No kidding," she said sarcastically. "I need a LOT of inspiration. I have publishers asking me when I'll start the next one, and not a single thought in my brain about what I could possibly write about."

"Well, we'll just have to fix that, won't we?" he laughed. "I'm sure you'll find a story. As I said, you're just worrying too much about everything because you need some rest. It's been a busy time at the vineyard, and with all your work and the books, you've barely had time to slow down."

"Oh, no, no, no," she said. "No slowing down for me. That's what my parents did and look at them now. They decided to slow down once, and they just got slower and slower and slower. Now, they both move at a snail's pace and drive us all nuts!"

"Here's an idea," Charles said sarcastically. "If you aren't finding what you're looking for in the old case files, then why don't you just make one up? Create a whole story from scratch. You can have as many twists and turns as your heart desires."

Avery sighed. "I tried, Charles. It didn't work. My imagination has become stagnant, I tell you."

"That's just not possible," Charles argued. "How can you say you have no imagination?"

"I sat for hours the other night trying to think of a new murder plot, and all I could think of were the cases I had just read through that morning in the old case files," she explained. "I could think of nothing new! Eventually, I got so frustrated I went to bed."

"You're tough to please, aren't you?" he teased.

Avery had a chuckle as she sipped her warm coffee. She looked down the street and saw that some of the shop workers were waiting to enter their shops, but still, the doors were all shut.

"Hey, listen, while I've got you on the line," Charles said. "See if you can't convince the cheese shop to stock some of your wine. What better place to sell wine than alongside cheese?"

"I'm way ahead of you," she said. "I've got a bottle in my bag for the owner to take home and taste. You don't know who owns this shop, do you?"

"No, sorry," Charles said. "I haven't been to that side of town in years. I go to the same three shops each week. That's how I've always done it, and that is probably how I will continue to do it until I die."

"Now you, my friend, are easy to please," Avery joked.

Charles and Avery had become friends since she'd taken over the vineyard. He worked in her wine room and did all the tastings. He was excellent at his job, but he was an even more excellent friend to her.

In general, he was somebody she could rely on. Having worked as a police officer in his life, Charles also had great respect for his work, which was a quality that she didn't always see in the other members of her staff. She had quickly learned that she could teach a new employee just about anything except work ethic. Contrary to popular belief, this was not a learnable skill. And thankfully for her, Charles had undeniable integrity to ensure a job well done. He sold so much wine each week that Avery genuinely worried about what would happen to her business if anything ever happened to him.

"Did you take the shiraz?" he asked. "We're selling that one like crazy lately. It must be the weather, but everybody wants a case of it. I'm almost tempted to fill it out on the order sheets in advance!"

"I'll be honest with you. I was in such a rush to leave the house this morning that I'm not sure which bottle I took. But I know it is some kind of a red," she said through laughter. "And it turns out that I didn't need to rush at all. None of these shops are even open yet!" she said.

"Are you sure?" Charles asked. "It seems like the time for them to have opened."

"Well, I'm looking down the street, and every door is still locked," Avery said. "I guess this side of Los Robles starts later in the day."

"Did you see that the bookstore is for sale?" Charles asked. "I'm considering buying the business. It's been around for so long, and it's pretty well-established. Then when I buy it, I can have an entire shelf just for your books."

"You can't buy the bookstore!" Avery argued. "I need you at the vineyard. You're the best employee I have there. If you leave me, I will never forgive you."

Charles laughed. "I was just going to buy it. Do you think I'm interested in selling books all day?"

"You sell wine all day," Avery said blankly.

"Yes, but wine is fun!" Charles said. "People come in here and sip and talk, and I learn about them. It's a social thing. Bookstores are always quiet, serious places. No, I'd hire people to run it for me, but it would be mine."

"I don't know...it seems like—"

She didn't have the chance to finish her sentence. Sprinkles had started tugging on his leash, and no matter how many times she gave him the signal to calm down, he refused. So she turned to see what had him so interested and saw that he was pushing open the door to the cheese shop with his nose.

"It's open!" she said to Charles. "I must have been so distracted with our conversation that I missed them unlocking it."

She had noticed that all the other shops in the street still remained shut and that the employees of those shops who waited outside seemed equally as confused about it as she was.

"Let me know what he says about the wine sales," Charles said excitedly.

Avery walked inside and came to a complete halt. It was so sudden that even on the other end of the line, Charles could tell that something was wrong.

"Avery?" he asked. "Is everything alright?"

"I don't think we're going to be selling wine here," Avery said with a shaky voice.

"What? Did you ask him already? What are you talking about?" Charles asked.

Avery swallowed hard. "I can't ask him anything," she said. "Because I'm looking at his dead body."

Visit https://a.co/d/hqMb0T6
to get *Murder at the Cheese Shop* now!

For a free book and to hear about upcoming releases, visit www.danisimms.com

Recipes

Puffy Pancake (serves 4)

4 tablespoons salted butter
4 large eggs
¼ teaspoon salt
1 cup all-purpose flour
1 cup whole or low fat milk
½ lemon, cut into wedges
Powdered sugar for dusting
Maple syrup, if desired

- Preheat oven to 425°F.
- Put butter in a 9x13 inch pan and into the oven as it is preheating (to melt).
- Combine the eggs, salt, flour, and milk in a medium-sized mixing bowl.
- Whisk the mixture to make a smooth batter.
- Pour the contents of the mixing bowl into the pan directly over melted butter.

- Bake for 15-20 minutes until the mixture puffs up and the top is slightly browned.
- Serve immediately, dusted with powdered sugar and lemon wedges (juiced over the pancake, to taste) on the side.

Excellent with fresh fruit, whipped cream, and sausages!

Pairing options: Earl Gray tea or Eiswein (ice wine)

Killer Grilled Cheese Sandwiches (serves 4)

2 tablespoons butter
8 tablespoons grated parmesan cheese
4 tablespoons fig jam
8 slices sourdough bread
16 slices of Swiss or gruyere cheese

- Heat pan to medium.
- Melt ½ tablespoon butter in pan.
- Spread 1 tablespoon of fig jam on the inside piece of sandwich bread.
- Sprinkle 2 tablespoons of parmesan cheese over butter in pan.
- Place two slices of bread open-face in the pan over parmesan (this will form the crusty goodness).
- Divide four slices of cheese over bread.
- Once the cheeses start to melt, assemble the sandwich.
- If the cheeses aren't melting fast enough as the crust browns, microwave sandwich for 30 seconds and finish on pan.
- Repeat with remaining ingredients.
- Serve with potato chips or tomato soup.

Pairing options: Sparkling white wine or ice-cold pale ale

Lasagna Soup (serves 6)

2 tablespoons olive oil, divided
1 pound ground beef (90% lean or higher)
1 large yellow onion, diced
4 garlic cloves, diced fine
4 cups chicken broth
1 can (14.5 ounces) crushed tomatoes
1 can (14.5 ounces) diced tomatoes
3 tablespoons tomato paste
2 teaspoons dried basil
1 teaspoon dried oregano
½ teaspoon dried rosemary
½ teaspoon dried thyme
Salt and freshly ground black pepper to taste
8 lasagna noodles
1 ½ cups mozzarella cheese, shredded
½ cup parmesan cheese, shredded fine
8 ounces ricotta cheese
2 tablespoons fresh parsley, chopped

- In a large pot over medium-high heat, add 1 tablespoon of oil.
- Brown ground beef and season with salt and pepper. Drain and set aside.
- In the same pot, add remaining oil and onion. Sauté until softened (3-4 minutes).
- Add garlic, sauté additional 30 seconds.
- Carefully pour in broth, tomatoes (both crushed and diced), tomato paste, dried herbs, and beef.
- Salt and pepper to taste.
- When the mixture starts to boil, reduce to medium-low heat.

- Cover and simmer for 25 minutes.
- Cook lasagna noodles per package instructions. Once cooked, cut into bite-sized pieces.
- In a medium bowl, prepare cheese mixtures by mixing mozzarella, parmesan, and ricotta cheeses.
- Add lasagna pieces to the pot of soup.
- Add chopped parsley.
- To serve, spoon soup into bowls and top with cheese mixture.

Pairing options: Cabernet Sauvignon or Amarone

A Different Kind of Lemon Bar (serves 6)

BAR INGREDIENTS

1 cup butter, softened
1 ¼ cups sugar
2 tablespoons lemon zest
4 eggs
2 tablespoons fresh lemon juice
1 ½ cups all-purpose flour
1 teaspoon baking powder

LEMON GLAZE INGREDIENTS

1 ¼ cups powdered sugar
4 tablespoons fresh lemon juice
5 tablespoons lemon zest

- Preheat the oven to 350°F.
- Prepare a 9×13 baking pan by lining with parchment paper.
- Whisk flour and baking powder together in a large mixing bowl.
- Beat together the butter, sugar, lemon juice, and zest with a hand or stand mixer until the mixture is light and fluffy.
- Add eggs one at a time and mix until combined.
- Slowly add flour and baking powder until combined.
- Pour batter into the baking pan
- Bake in the oven for 25-30 minutes. Test with a toothpick (should come out with few crumbs).
- Cool completely in the pan.

- To make the glaze, whisk powdered sugar, lemon juice, and zest in a large bowl until smooth.
- Spread glaze over warm lemon bars.

It'll be tempting, but be sure to allow the glaze to set up overnight!

Pairing options: Oaked chardonnay or limoncello